A Little Night Matchmaking

A Little Night Matchmaking

Debrah Morris

THORNDIKE
CHIVERS

This Large Print edition is published by Thorndike Press®, Waterville, Maine USA and by BBC Audiobooks Ltd, Bath, England.

Published in 2005 in the U.S. by arrangement with Harlequin Books S.A.

Published in 2005 in the U.K. by arrangement with Harlequin Mills & Boon II B.V. 20033343

U.S. Hardcover 0-7862-7906-0 (Romance)
U.K. Hardcover 1-4056-3504-5 (Chivers Large Print)
U.K. Softcover 1-4056-3505-3 (Camden Large Print)

MORAY COUNCIL
LIBRARIES &
INFORMATION SERVICES

The text of this Large Print edition is unabridged.
Other aspects of the book may vary from the original edition.

Set in 16 pt. Plantin by Ramona Watson.

Printed in the United States on permanent paper.

British Library Cataloguing-in-Publication Data available

Library of Congress Cataloging-in-Publication Data

Morris, Debrah.
   A little night matchmaking / by Debrah Morris.
      p. cm. — (Thorndike Press large print romance)
   ISBN 0-7862-7906-0 (lg. print : hc : alk. paper)
   1. Large type books. I. Title. II. Thorndike Press large print romance series.
PS3613.O7723L58 2005
813'.6—dc22
                                         2005013688

Emerson said, "The glory of friendship is not the outstretched hand, nor the kindly smile, nor the joy of companionship; it's the spiritual inspiration that comes to one when he discovers that someone else believes in him and is willing to trust him with his friendship."

Willie Ferguson, friend, critique partner and road trip companion. Thank you for nearly twenty years of laughter, understanding, support and inspiration. Thanks for trusting me with your friendship.

Chloe's Favorite Snickerdoodles

$1/2$ cup butter, softened
$1/2$ cup shortening
1 $1/2$ cups white sugar
2 eggs
2 tsp vanilla extract
2 $3/4$ cups all-purpose flour
2 tsp cream of tartar
1 tsp baking soda
$1/4$ tsp salt
2 tbsp white sugar
2 tsp ground cinnamon

1. Tell a grown-up to turn on the oven and set it at 400°F.

2. Smoosh together butter, shortening, 1 $1/2$ cups sugar, eggs and vanilla extract and mix it all up good. Stir flour, cream of tartar, baking soda and salt together in another bowl and then add the powdery stuff to the creamy stuff. Roll the dough into balls about an inch big. (Mommy says if the dough is too sticky to handle, you can put it in the fridge for a few minutes first.)

3. Mix 2 tablespoons sugar and 2 teaspoons cinnamon. Roll balls of dough

around in mixture until you can't see any dough. Place the balls 2 inches apart on big ungreased baking sheets. Whatever you do, don't put the balls too close together. *Very* important!

4. Put them in the oven and help clean up the mess while you're waiting. They only have to bake 8 to 10 minutes, or until lightly browned. These are 'sposed to be soft cookies, so watch 'em so they don't get too brown or too hard. Remove immediately from baking sheets to wire racks. Makes about 4 dozen cookies, unless you eat too much dough while you're rolling.

Prologue

The After Place

"Please, don't send me back to earth!" Celestian was really in trouble this time. He had finally gone too far. Tampered with The Plan once too often. He'd already been busted down from time-out monitor to prayer courier, and yet here he was again, facing a Level Three Penalty Hearing. Would he ever learn to straighten up and fly right?

"A decision has been made." He couldn't see the hallowed faces of the Panel's senior saints, but their voices resonated from three different directions.

He couldn't go back. Earth was a dangerous place. "It's been over three hundred years, Your Excellencies. I am unfit to live again."

A calm, sonorous voice filled the interview chamber's white space. "You shan't be given an earthly life, Celestian. You must retain spirit form."

"If I may speak freely —"

"You may not speak at all." Another voice. Deeper. Not so calm. "Listen and obey. We do not wish to see you in Judicial Chambers."

"Yes, sirs." Nor did he wish to be *seen* in Judicial Chambers.

"More than once you have failed to follow After Place policy." Another voice seemed determined to point out the obvious.

"Perhaps I've behaved imprudently, but —"

"Your imprudence borders on insubordination," St. Cranky snapped. "You have placed us in an untenable position."

"You have lost sight of your purpose," St. Obvious intoned.

"We trust a lesson in humility will teach you to respect The Plan." Even St. Calm didn't sound so calm now.

"An example must be set." St. Cranky, of course.

"Yes, sirs. But banning me to earth seems harsh in light of —"

"Do not consider yourself banned." St. Calm recovered his equanimity. "Consider your return to earth a mission."

"A mission? Me?" Celestian squeaked. What in heaven's name were they thinking? He did not possess the skills required for Earthwork.

"Celestial beings are never given assignments they cannot fulfill," St. Calm reminded.

"Very well." Celestian sighed. There was no arguing with a Review Panel. "I can't wait to hear what I must do."

"That's the spirit!" St. Obvious didn't understand sarcasm. "Since you are guilty of manipulating circumstances for your own purpose, you shall be given ample opportunity to do so by returning to earth as a guide."

"A spirit guide?" Celestian dared to hope. That wasn't so bad. "Whose earthly life must I guide?"

"Your human's name is Chloe Mitchum."

Celestian's optimism faded as memories of Slapdown, Texas flooded back. "But Chloe Mitchum is a child."

"Yes, an old soul who recently entered the fifth year of her current life. Helping an innocent little girl won't strain your limited resources, will it?"

"No, sir." Celestian listened as the Panel explained he was to befriend a child experiencing earthly problems. What problems did a five-year-old have?

"All you have to do is provide comfort, succor and guidance. The usual."

He could do that. "As in, look both

ways before you cross the street. Brush your teeth up and down *and* back and forth. Drink your milk. That kind of guidance?"

"Your primary objective will be helping Chloe's mother meet her soul mate," said St. Cranky.

"What?" Matchmaking was definitely not in his toolbox.

"Nothing complicated. Assist them in falling in love. Facilitate their courtship. Insure their lifelong happiness, a fate already slated for them. That is all." St. Calm's impossibly reasonable tone frustrated Celestian.

"You lost me at courtship." He knew nothing about making people fall in love. He'd died without ever experiencing the emotion.

"Despite the combined efforts of several departments," St. Obvious continued, "we have been unable to bring these two soul mates together. Their paths have paralleled, but have not crossed."

"Time is running out," added St. Calm. "She married the wrong man once and is overcautious. He has stubbornly vowed to remain a bachelor."

Celestian began to sense how truly difficult his task would be.

"Extreme measures are needed. That's

where you come in," said St. Obvious. "We require regular progress reports, so stop by Central Supply before you leave and pick up a H.A.R.P."

"A harp, sir?"

"Handheld Analog Reporting Pad," St. Obvious explained. "The new technology far surpasses the old. Very user-friendly."

"If you succeed in helping the soul mates find true love, you may return to your former position in the time-out room." St. Cranky dangled the bait.

"And if I fail?" Celestian asked.

"If you fail, you are stuck." Leave it to St. Obvious. "Stuck on earth. Stuck in Texas. Stuck with Chloe."

Doomed. As were the humans if he was their best shot at happiness. "I don't understand. Why do soul mates destined for eternal love need my help?"

Silence filled the interview chamber as the panel conferred with one another. St. Cranky finally spoke. "Due to a system error, these two soul mates currently occupy Antipodean Mortal Coils."

"Anti what?" Celestian wasn't up on the jargon. He'd never expected to wind up on happily-ever-after detail.

A babble of no longer serene voices boomed through the chamber.

"Opposites. Contrary in personality, temperament and values," explained St. Calm.

"Totally and hopelessly mismatched," added St. Obvious.

"You call that a glitch?" Celestian began to sense how hopeless his mission really was. "Try problem of mammoth proportions."

"Dear boy, do not be discouraged. If you wish to return to The After Place, you mustn't let the fact that the subjects have absolutely nothing in common deter you from your worthy goal." St. Cranky had suddenly become St. Smug.

He knew Celestian didn't have a prayer.

Chapter One

Love is the only fire hot enough
To melt the iron obstinacy
of a creature's will

— Anonymous

Unknown and uninvited, he had slipped into her bedroom again last night. Not quite real enough to be frightening, his arrival wasn't entirely unexpected. Three times now, he'd appeared in the darkest hour of the night. At first, he had stood quietly at the foot of her bed and said nothing. He seemed to await an invitation, but she could hardly offer one. She couldn't speak or move or beckon. She could only bide.

The tall stranger was oddly familiar, though there was shadow where his face should be. When he finally spoke, his whispered words were faint, as though drifting across a great, windy chasm. When she didn't answer, he disappeared, but she ached for his return.

The next night, he became bolder. He

sat on the bed beside her, so close his comforting presence invaded her senses and paralyzed her with pleasure. His voice was stronger than before, like distant thunder gaining power as a storm approached. He murmured, *Brandy, Brandy, Brandy,* turning her name into a song.

Last night when the stranger appeared in her room, he knelt beside her bed and touched her cheek. His dark head bent close, and his warm breath bathed her skin with need. Desperate to feel his lips on hers, she tried to turn her head, but couldn't. She could only sense and feel and hear. He whispered a yearning expression of love in her ear. *Brandy. Don't sleepwalk through life. Wake up.*

And so she had, to an empty bedroom filled with gray morning light, echoes of regret and the faint scent of cinnamon.

Brandy Mitchum squinted as her eyes readjusted to the bright afternoon sunlight and tamped down memories of the troubling dreams. She steered her old car down the washboard country road. She was running late. If Harry Peet hadn't insisted on reading the thick sheaf of legal documents before signing, her mind wouldn't have had so much time to wander. To dwell. She had to focus. The Midnight Man might be ruining her sleep on a recurring basis, but she couldn't let him interfere with work. Futterman wouldn't accept less than her best.

She glanced at her watch. The unscheduled trip to the Milk of Human Kindness Dairy had chomped a two-hour chunk out of her afternoon. Time was tight, but if no additional glitches arose, she could still hustle back to Odessa in time to pick up Chloe from the after-school program.

Her stomach rumbled. No lunch. She just couldn't seem to break that darned three-meal-a-day habit. Hoping to find candy stashed in her oversize mommy purse, she kept her eyes on the road and fished among the jumble of Happy Meal toys, moist towelettes and clean size five Powerpuff Girls underwear. The catch of the day was a Hershey bar that had succumbed to heatstroke, but what the heck? A sugar hit was a sugar hit. Steering with one hand, she opened the wrapper and licked warm goo off the paper.

Melting as fast as the chocolate, Brandy switched on the air conditioner, but the fan grumbled and blew hot humid air in her face. Mid-September, and the outside temperature hovered near ninety. Not a good day for the A/C to conk. But then, *no* day in West Texas was a good day to lose climate control. She cranked down the window and leaned across the seat to lower the glass in the passenger door. Might as well roast evenly on both sides.

"Hey, lady! Wake up!"

She glanced up at the shouted warning and expelled a curse that would never have escaped her lips had her five-year-old daughter been present. She pumped the brakes, and the car slid in loose gravel before skidding to a teeth-rattling stop. The shoulder restraint locked in, preventing a close encounter between her head and the steering wheel.

Disaster averted. Barely. If the car had skidded another yard, it would have struck the truck angled across the road. Brandy sucked in a deep breath to calm her pounding heart.

A tall man in a black Stetson and mirrored sunglasses yelled as he approached. "What's the matter with you, lady? You asleep?"

Not exactly. She'd been daydreaming about a nighttime dream, and the distraction had almost gotten her killed.

When she didn't answer, the man stooped down and scowled at close range. "You nearly hit my trailer."

"I noticed." A large truck pulling a flatbed loaded with heavy equipment had failed to negotiate the turn onto the narrow country road. The dual wheels on the trailer's left side had slid into the rocky ditch beside the road, blocking entry onto the highway. Four men stood in the sun as though awaiting orders from the scowler.

"You all right?" Stetson's words couldn't have contained less concern. "Not hurt, are you?"

"No. Scared spitless, but the condition isn't fatal." Brandy noticed the logo spelled out in big flaming letters on the side of the truck. Hotspur Well Control. Now there was a fine piece of small-world rotten luck. She had almost plowed into a truck owned by the very company her boss was suing on Harry Peet's behalf. At least she didn't feel too bad about the litigation. The company *was* a nuisance, and its employees weren't exactly courteous, either.

"Then I'd appreciate it if you'd get out of the way so my men can hook a mini-crane to that trailer."

"Sure. No problem." Her heart rate returned to normal, but every time the man spoke, it kicked up again. There was something familiar about that voice. When Brandy shifted the car into reverse, it

19

coughed like an asthmatic senior citizen, then rattled and died. She groaned. Not now. She couldn't afford a tune-up until payday. *Please, please, please start.*

Muttering a prayer to the patron saint of old engines, she performed her standard good luck ritual. Three taps on the dash. Rearview mirror realign. Kiss blown in the direction of Chloe's picture swinging from her key chain.

"Today would be good," Stetson grumbled.

"Fine!" When she tried again the engine wheezed to life. Thank you, St. Combustion. She backed the car several yards, churning up enough dirt to make the tall man cough. Served him right for snapping her head off. He hadn't bothered removing the aviator-style sunglasses, and the wide hat brim cast his face in shadows. She couldn't get a good look at his face, but the rest of him wasn't too bad. Of course, the state was full of hunky cowboys.

This one had a major case of the four Ts.

Tall. Tan. Tough. Texan.

He stomped off without another word, his scuffed boots kicking up angry little clouds of dust. Add a fifth T. Testy. Brandy watched him walk away. There was something familiar about the set of his wide shoulders. Had they met before? No. She'd remember him. Confidence without swagger. Firm step. Slim hips. Faded jeans hugging all the right places. She would definitely remember.

Close but no cigar. She didn't need another difficult man in her life and wasn't willing to go there. Following her divorce four years ago, her mother had warned her about dating again. "Be careful you don't come down with frog-kiss fever." She'd explained the condition whereby a woman feels compelled to give even unsuitable men a chance in the hopes of finding the right one. Well, not her. She was holding out for Prince Charming. Only nice guys need apply.

Brandy parked at the side of the road, got out and leaned against her car in the slanting afternoon sun. She used her cell phone to call the law office and let the receptionist know where she was and why. Then she punched in the number for the after-school program. They had a strict tardy policy and every minute past six o'clock would cost her. Still, she should warn them she might be late. Chloe was such a worrier.

After making the calls, she waited impatiently as the men unhitched the disabled trailer from the truck. The flat, dry pastureland wasn't much to look at, but Stetson had plenty of eye appeal. Too bad he didn't have a personality to match. If he weren't so bossy, his deep voice might have been sexy. If he weren't so fiercely masculine, his long-legged, loose-hipped stride might have been graceful. There was economy in his movements. This was a man who didn't waste time or energy. Such intensity would make him equally at home in a brawl or on a dance floor. In the boardroom or the bedroom.

Disgusted with her errant thoughts, Brandy removed her suit jacket and tossed it in the back seat. The inside of the car was roughly the temperature of a pottery kiln. Sunstroke would explain why she was having feverish thoughts about a stranger who couldn't work up enough interest to glance her way. Which was worse? Daytime delusions or nocturnal fantasies? No doubt, both were side effects of self-inflicted celibacy. Four years was a long time to be alone.

She glanced at her watch and groaned. The afternoon was slipping away. She'd never get to town by six if she didn't hit the road soon.

"Hey, mister!"

The man in the black Stetson looked up. "Yeah?"

She held out her arm and jabbed her wristwatch. "How much longer is this going to take?"

"As long as it takes." He shook his head as though she'd just asked a stupid question and turned his back on her.

Twenty minutes later, the crane hoisted the trailer back onto the road. It took the crew another ten minutes to clear the equipment. Brandy jumped behind the wheel and started the engine, and this time it didn't even grumble. The boss waved her around with an exaggerated bow, but stepped in front of the car at the last minute.

"Now what?" The engine idled like a threshing machine, and she clutched the vibrating steering wheel.

He walked around the car to the driver's side window. "Timing needs adjusting."

"No kidding. Life is all about timing. And yours isn't all that hot." Even if the rest of him was.

"I meant your car's running a little rough."

He had stopped her to point out the obvious? "Thanks, I'll get right on it." She let up on the brake.

He slapped the roof of her car. "Wait. Something else needs fixing before you head back to town."

She gave the righted trailer a pointed look. "Haven't you already done what you came for?"

"Not quite." He pulled a red bandana from the back pocket of his jeans, reached into the car and scrubbed at her cheek.

"What are you doing?" Brandy wasn't the screeching type, but his unexpected action startled her. Even more startling, was her *reaction*. Without warning, the stranger's touch slammed past the barricade she'd erected around her emotions since her divorce. He touched more than her cheek. Tapping into an undercurrent of longing, the connection flattened her defenses like an eighteen-wheeler rolling over a traffic cone.

The rush of odd feelings shook Brandy to the core, but not as much as the effort required to conceal them. Just as she began to recover from the impact, another startling thought blindsided her.

She knew this man.

The notion pierced Brandy's mind, strong and certain. She'd seen him before. Somewhere. Sometime. Hadn't she? No. He was definitely a stranger. And an annoying one at that. Still, she couldn't deny the uneasy sense of having been touched by him before. She gripped the steering wheel tightly, forgetting for a moment how to drive. Instinct told her to step on the gas, yet she couldn't resist the dangerous urge to stay. Distracted, she gunned the engine. She was light-headed and dizzy, but that was due to the sun's heat, not the man's.

"Next time you eat chocolate on a warm day," he said with the twitch of a smile, "check the mirror for leftovers." He waited five pounding heartbeats before wheeling around and striding back to his men.

Brandy stared after him, but he was intent on his work and didn't give her another look. What an unsettling encounter. She sped away feeling ridiculous but couldn't stop thinking about him on the drive back to town. Understandable. It had been a long time since a man had rattled her so badly.

Long time? Try never. The freaky been-there-done-that sensation inspired by Stetson's touch was the strongest example of déjà vu she'd ever experienced. Sleeping emotions rumbled, stirring to life like a volcano that had been dormant too long.

Was this what love at first sight felt like? Or, in this case, love at first *swipe?* Ridiculous. She didn't believe in anything so un-realistic, nor did she trust the swoon factor. She'd picked one husband based on runaway chemistry, and hadn't that turned out great? She was older now. Wise enough to know better. She and Joe had spent two unhappy years together, and only one sweet thing had come from their doomed marriage. Chloe.

Her precocious, imaginative daughter's head was often in the clouds, which meant Mommy had to keep her feet planted firmly on the ground. As strangely thrilling as that split second encounter on the road had been, she would probably never lay eyes on the guy again.

There was nothing mysterious about what had happened. Too much sun, not enough lunch and a dehydrated libido ex-plained her crazy reaction.

Brandy pulled into the school's turn-around driveway at three minutes past six, left the car running and hurried into the cafeteria to the after-school program. "Sorry I'm late, Amy. I was stuck in a jam."

"No problem." The college student in charge put away the broom.

Chloe placed the picture book she'd been reading in a big plastic tub. "Stuck in jam? That's funny, Mommy. You mean like grape jam?"

"No, silly. Traffic jam. A truck was blocking the road." Brandy reached into her purse. "How much do I owe you?"

Amy helped Chloe with her backpack. "Nothing. I couldn't have left any sooner. Let's call it even this time."

"Are you sure?"

"Positive. Chloe, you're a good helper. Would you straighten the books so the lid will fit on the tub?" Once the child's attention was engaged, Amy took Brandy aside. "I need to ask you about Chloe's new friend."

"Which new friend?"

"The invisible one. She's been talking to him a lot lately. I was wondering how you want me to handle the situation?"

Brandy was unaware of any situation in need of handling. "This is the first I've heard of an invisible friend."

"Chloe spends a lot of time playing alone instead of interacting with the other kids. She carries on whole conversations with an imaginary playmate." Amy lowered her voice. "Today I heard her saying she didn't need his help. Said she had kindergarten under control. She has a great vocabulary, by the way."

27

"Yes, I know." Pride replaced worry. "She tested out at the ninth-grade level in receptive and seventh-grade in expressive. Her IQ is above average, too. Did you know she taught herself to read last year using two packs of sight cards and a stack of Dr. Seuss books?"

"She's an incredible little girl."

"She's very creative. I'm sure the pretend playmate is just another figment of her imagination," Brandy suggested.

"I learned in my child psychology class that the creation of an imaginary world isolates a child from the real one. It can be the sign of a deeper problem."

"Really?" Brandy's empty stomach clenched with worry. Why hadn't she thought of that?

"She got a little upset today. I overheard her telling her 'friend' to go away, which might mean something. She said school was a kid's job, and if he kept hanging around he would get her fired."

Brandy winced. Chloe knew all about that. Brandy had lost two jobs because of childcare conflicts. "Thank you for sharing your concerns, Amy. I appreciate the time and attention you give Chloe."

"She's a joy. I hope I'm not out of line, but I talked to Megan, the other caregiver, and she didn't know what to do, either."

Brandy patted the girl's arm. "You're not out of line. Chloe is obviously having more trouble adjusting to the move than I thought. Thanks for letting me know."

Amy nodded. "New town. New house. New school. Lots of changes."

"The pace was much slower back home. Now she has to get up early for before-school care, spend all day in the gifted-and-talented kindergarten and stay for after-school care, too."

"I can so identify. I have three part-time jobs and a full course load at Odessa College. Okay for me, but stressful for a five-year-old."

Doubt flooded Brandy's stomach with a tsunami acid wave. Had she traumatized Chloe by abandoning their familiar world to start over in a strange city? She'd made hard choices recently. What if they had been the wrong ones?

Her boss, Mr. Futterman, didn't think a woman with a child could devote a hundred percent of her energy to work. Naively she had hoped a career with real earning potential would be her ticket out of the nickel-and-dime job world, but she'd had another reason for putting herself through paralegal school.

She wanted to accomplish something worthwhile. After years as a deadbeat dad, her ex-husband had finally gotten his act together. He'd been elected county sheriff back home and now paid child support regularly. He'd fallen hard for the local doctor and was happily married. She didn't begrudge Joe his newfound contentment. She was happy for him. Everyone should be lucky enough to find true love once in a lifetime.

Joe's success had inspired her to do more. To be more. His marriage to Mallory Peterson had given her hope. Maybe there was a special person in the world for her, too.

"Mommy?" Chloe tugged on her sleeve. "Can we go?"

Brandy took her daughter's small hand. "I won't be late again, Amy. Thank you for bringing the 'situation' to my attention."

Brandy stopped by the ATM to get money for the dry cleaning and gas. As she placed the bills in her purse, a familiar white pickup truck turned the corner and caught her attention. She couldn't see the driver's face, but the wide shoulders were unmistakable. So was the flaming logo on the door.

Hotspur Well Control.

Chloe piped up from the back seat. "I'm hot."

"I know, baby. The air conditioner stopped working."

"How come?"

"Just old, I guess."

"As old as me?"

Brandy laughed. "Much older than you." Weird. Their paths had crossed again. Glimpsing him revved up all the emotions she'd suppressed, but she tried not to think about him while picking up her clothes at the cleaners. Like the dreams that haunted her, their encounter was hard to forget. She'd felt a sense of portent at his touch. What if she hadn't seen the last of him? She laughed. Chloe wasn't the only one with an overactive imagination. Seeing the sexy stranger again was a coincidence. Nothing more.

A few minutes later at the gas station, she had to wonder. She parked alongside an available pump just as the same white pickup pulled away from the one next to her. The driver stopped at the street, his large, competent hands resting on the wheel, and watched for a break in traffic.

Hotspur Well Control again. Who was stalking whom here? She started pumping gas but stared in the tinted driver's side window over the top of her car. The man

31

in the black Stetson startled her by turning around and staring back. He lowered his sunglasses for a better look, but the traffic cleared, another motorist honked and he drove away.

It wasn't so strange to run into the same guy three times in one afternoon. Awareness was like that. When she'd first become pregnant, she'd noticed other pregnant women everywhere she went. Driving a purple car made her notice other purple cars. Nothing weird about that. Just human nature.

The sun was sinking fast by the time Brandy finished her errands and headed home. The day had lasted too long, and Supermom was super tired. Poor little Chloe had to be worn-out too.

"You're awfully quiet, punkin." Brandy glanced in the rearview mirror and smiled at her daughter strapped into a booster seat, her blond bangs plastered to her forehead by baby sweat. "Everything all right?"

"Yep. Just thinking."

Like mother, like daughter. "When you get the problems of the universe sorted out, will you let me know?"

"Okay, Mommy."

She shouldn't worry. Chloe was deeper than most children her age, more sensitive. All kids had active imaginations. An invisible playmate was her daughter's way of coping with the new stressors in her life. They'd have a nice talk over dinner, and she'd make sure Chloe understood the difference between real and imaginary.

Tonight she would prepare a real sit-down, we're-a-family meal served on plates instead of from takeout bags. Country fried chicken fingers, mashed potatoes minus the yucky gravy, steamed baby carrots cut in tiny rounds and chocolate pudding. All of Chloe's favorite foods. A surefire way to earn mommy points.

Four blocks from home the cell phone rang. Brandy groaned when she read Futterman's name on caller ID. She didn't have to answer. It was after seven o'clock. She was a paralegal, not an indentured servant. She'd given the firm nearly eleven hours today. She was tired. Her child was hungry. She had a life outside Futterman-Ulbright.

And the salary Fenton Futterman paid her financed that life. Well, put it that way. She took the call and listened as her frantic employer explained his latest problem. He had an early pretrial conference in the morning and had somehow lost the documents she'd meticulously prepared from sketchy notes and marginalia. Her hopes for a quiet evening flew out the window. Her boss considered motherhood a disability. He wouldn't consider chocolate pudding a good excuse.

Nor was he willing to find the file on her computer and print another copy. She'd have to return to the office. The task wouldn't take long, but it would cut into time she wanted to spend with Chloe.

Would forfeiting mommy points earn her a few employee points? She glanced into the back seat. She was working hard to give Chloe the kind of life she deserved, but it wasn't really fair to drag her along for the ride. On the other hand, she couldn't afford to tell her demanding boss no.

Life was a series of trade-offs. Balance was the key.

"Don't worry, Mr. Futterman. I'm on it." She disconnected the call and released an exhausted sigh. The scales were tipping and Mommy was losing.

H.A.R.P. Field Report
From: Celestian, Earthbound Operative
To: Mission Control
Re: Operation True Love

Current Objective: Contact human ally and introduce matchmaking protocol. Initiate communication between male and female subjects and assess their respective relationship skills.

Progress Notes: Contact with child established. Screening tests reveal depth of subjects' differences. Limited success with current objective. Male subject exhibits resistance to operative's environmental manipulation techniques. Measurements indicate commitment levels below acceptable standards.

Female subject emotionally accessible and responsive to dream therapy. Exhibits interest in long-term commitment but is currently distracted by vocational duress. Internal stress and external pressure reduce suggestibility and make her less susceptible to covert tactics.

Plan: Initiate emotional retraining of subjects and increase contact between them.

Personal Assessment: Operative desperately lacks experience to complete this mission and respectfully requests to be relieved of duty.

Chapter Two

Brandy pulled into the fast-food drive-thru and ordered the usual. With the food cooling on the seat beside her, she drove downtown against rush hour traffic, an exhausted salmon swimming upstream without even the prospect of mating to motivate her.

By the time she arrived at the office, the firm was closed for the day. All the smart people had gone home. Juggling her brief-case and purse in one hand and the bag of food in the other, she unlocked the dead bolt and ushered Chloe inside. The lever jammed when she tried to relock the door. The universe was conspiring against her today. She pulled the knob and jiggled the catch to secure the door and led Chloe to her small office at the back of the building.

"Is this your work?" Chloe looked around curiously. She hadn't visited the hallowed halls of Futterman-Ulbright before.

"Yep. Sorry you had to come down here,

honey. Mommy needs to get some papers ready for her boss."

"I know. They got losted." Chloe peered at the computer monitor's space-themed screen saver, then swiveled the desk chair in dizzying circles.

"Right." She hadn't mentioned the missing papers. "How did you —"

"Your boss should be more careful."

"I agree." She cleared a spot on a corner of the desk and set out a colorful cardboard box. Cinnamon. Again. Where was that coming from? Brandy found nothing unusual among the meal's contents. She sniffed the air near Chloe where the scent was strongest. Ah, cinnamon crackers. "Here you go. You can eat while I work."

Chloe wasn't happy with her meal and went straight for the toy. "Oh, ratties. I already have this one." Unwrapping the burger, she carefully removed both pickles and picked off every microscopic bit of onion before dumping French fries on the wrapper.

"Sorry, baby." Trying not to feel too guilty about all the fast-food meals they'd eaten recently, Brandy poked a straw in the milk carton. She squirted a packet of ketchup in a neat red pile, careful not to let the condiment touch the fries. Chloe had a thing about mixing food. She preferred to dip.

"That's all right, Mommy." She tore the wrapping off the disappointing toy and laid it aside. "I can start a collection."

Sipping her super-size diet cola, Brandy sat at the computer and pulled up the file containing the case documents her boss needed for the conference. She couldn't believe someone as anal as Futterman could misplace something so important. Moving anything on his desk an eighth of an inch left or right resulted in a major freak-out. Today's weirdness just kept piling up. And it wasn't Friday *or* the thirteenth.

Deciding to make a spare this time, she set the printer control for two copies and started the process.

"So, baby, can I ask you something?"

"Sure, Mommy."

She blotted a dot of ketchup from her daughter's mouth with a paper napkin. "Do you think school is a kid's job?"

"Uh-huh. Like being a pair of legals is your job."

"Right." She smiled. "Amy says you have a new friend. Tell me about her."

Chloe's dark brown eyes seemed much older in her baby face. "It's a him. His name is Celestian." She blended the four syllables together into two. Sles-chun.

Ah, Celestian. She'd heard the unusual name before. "Your dad's dog?"

"No. It's a different Celestian. He's supposed to help me, but most of the time I don't need any help and he gets his feelings hurted. I told him to go home today." Chloe rolled her eyes. "It's kindergarten, not college. He's too sensitive."

Brandy nodded. "Can you see Celestian?"

Chloe gave her a look she would have considered insulting had it come from anyone but a five-year-old. " 'Course I can."

"Can I?"

Chloe laughed and dipped another fry. "Nope. He's inbisible. He says I'm the only one who can see him."

"So you named your pretend friend after the little white dog that sleeps on your bed when you visit Daddy?"

Chloe's blond bob swung in vehement denial. "*I* didn't name him. That's his real name. And he's not pretend. He's real too. He's just inbisible to people who don't need to see him."

"He talks to you?" Brandy didn't know whether to be worried or relieved. On one hand, it was unsettling to think her daughter could 'see' invisible people, but on the other, the child's fantasy was probably just a way to personalize the little dog she missed.

What was her fantasy all about? Was the man who visited her dreams the personification of *her* own secret longings?

"Yep. Sometimes he talks too much. He's funny." She sobered. "He said other people wouldn't understand about him. Let's don't talk about it."

Was Chloe afraid to share feelings? Did she think her mother wouldn't understand or care? She'd never kept secrets before. Doubt settled on Brandy, weighing her down. Motherhood had never been easy, but she had managed, even without Joe's help. This problem was more complicated than making sure Chloe ate enough protein and got her vaccinations on time. Brandy had no more idea how to handle an invisible playmate than the girl at the after-school program. At least Amy had taken a child psychology class.

The printer continued to spit pages, the noise loud in the quiet office. Distracted by her thoughts, Brandy helped herself to a French fry. "We're buddies, punkin.

Powerpuff Girls. We don't keep secrets from each other."

"I know. This isn't a real secret." Chloe fingered the plastic toy. Made Barbie do a dance. "More like . . . private."

"I understand. What do you and Celestian talk about?"

Chloe took a bite of her baby burger, chewed and dutifully swallowed before speaking. "Stuff." She picked up another French fry, dunked it in ketchup and extended the dripping offering.

Chloe laughed when Brandy snapped up the fry with a wolfish growl. Maybe Chloe wasn't any more upset about the move than she had a right to be. Children were resilient. Brandy had not studied child psychology, but she knew that much. It wasn't unusual for a bright child to have an imaginary playmate. And parents often worried about things long after children had forgotten them.

If Chloe had invented Celestian because her mother was preoccupied with work, well, she'd fix that. She'd spend more time with her. Quality time. Do everything she could to make her daughter feel safe and loved. It was probably no coincidence that the playmate was male and named after Joe's dog. Maybe Chloe

41

missed her father more than Brandy realized.

After nearly three years of benign neglect
and indifference, Joe Mitchum had finally
taken his parental responsibilities seriously.
A near-death experience with a bolt of
lightning had jump-started his daddy engine, and he and Chloe had finally forged a
good relationship. Unfortunately Chloe
saw her father less since the move to
Odessa. Creating an imaginary Celestian
was probably her way of bringing a little
bit of her old home to her new one.

She understood the feeling. Something
was missing from her own life as well. A
quiet gentle man who shared her values. A
true partner to love her and Chloe and put
their interests first.

Now where had that thought come
from? She could make a life for her and
her daughter on her own, thank you. She
didn't need a man. If the right one came
along, so be it. If not, well, maybe it wasn't
meant to be.

"What stuff do you and Celestian talk
about?" Brandy turned her wandering attention back to Chloe.

"Getting along stuff. Being happy stuff.
But mostly trick stuff."

"Tricks? What kind of tricks?" Chloe

wasn't the type of child to test boundaries with misbehavior and blame it on the imaginary friend.

"You'll see." Chloe sipped her milk. She cocked her head to one side again as though tuned in to a voice Brandy couldn't hear. After a moment, she said, "Can we not talk about Celestian anymore?"

"Okay. But you'll let me know if you have a problem, won't you?"

Chloe's sunny face lit up with a wide grin. "I don't have problems, Mommy. I'm only five, remember?"

"Yes, I remember." The powerful scent of cinnamon permeated the room, and an unsettling sense of expectancy set Brandy's nerves on edge. Maybe it was the strange encounter with Stetson on the road today that had her twitching. She'd never been into new age ideas or dream analysis or anything that wasn't totally down to earth. So why couldn't she shake the feeling that something life-altering was about to happen? "Honey, is Celestian here now?"

After a long pause, Chloe nodded.

"Where?" Brandy's gaze darted around the room. The suite of offices was empty. The rest of the staff had gone home, and the cleaning people had not yet arrived. Outside on the street, traffic had thinned

43

out. Night had settled over Texas like a dark, smothering blanket.

Chloe slowly lifted her hand and pointed. "Right over there."

Of course, no one was perched atop the file cabinet, but Brandy looked anyway. The invisible playmate was a figment of her daughter's overactive imagination. Still, gooseflesh rose on her arms at the thought of another presence in the room. She squinted, playing along with Chloe's game. "Hmm. I can't see him. What does he look like?"

"Just regular."

"Is he a little boy? As big as you?"

"Nope. Grown-up size."

"Old? Or young?"

"He says he's three hundred and twenty-two," Chloe whispered in a conspiratorial tone. "But he doesn't look even as old as Grandpa."

Brandy marveled at Chloe's creativity. What had she ever done to deserve such a special child? "Does he have hair?"

" 'Course!" Chloe laughed again. "It's yellow and longer than yours. And his eyes are blue. He wears white clothes and no shoes."

Apparently, Celestian was very real to Chloe. She'd gone to great lengths to in-

44

vent details about his appearance. Brandy stroked her daughter's soft round cheek. "Punkin, is everything all right at school?"

Chloe's narrow shoulders lifted in an eloquent shrug. "Well, the teacher does her best with what she has to work with."

Brandy smiled. Where did she pick up that stuff? Chloe preferred her own company to that of other children and never minded playing alone. Still, niggling worry refused to die. "What about your classmates? Do you get along with them?"

"I guess so. We don't have much in common. They're pretty young. Most of them can't even read."

"They're the same age as you," Brandy pointed out.

Chloe nodded. "I know, but they act like *little* kids."

"They *are* little kids."

Chloe rolled her eyes. "Just 'cause they're five, doesn't mean they have to act five."

"True."

Had her daughter ever been a baby? Mothering Chloe had been one surprise after another. Dissatisfied with the inefficiency of crawling, she had walked at nine months. In an effort to communicate, she developed her own system of sign language at ten months. By eighteen months, she was speaking in intelligible sentences. Impatient to wait for school, she taught herself to read at four and a half.

Every morning before the mad dash out the door, logical, organized Chloe made sure Brandy had everything she needed for the day. Exhibiting an intriguing combination of wisdom and innocence, her daughter had always been advanced for her age. Not only did she march to a different drummer, she followed a beat most people couldn't even hear.

They finished their fast-food dinner in silence. Chloe didn't mention Celestian again, but a creepy, uneasy feeling set Brandy's nerves on edge. She needed to get out of the deserted office. Things would seem more normal once she got home. She tossed the food wrappers into the trash and gathered up her things as the printer finished the document.

Turning, she spotted a tall man standing in the open doorway, his broad shoulders nearly filling the space. She yelped in startled alarm. "Who the heck are you?"

"He came! He really came!" Chloe clapped her hands and jumped up and down, as though she'd been awaiting the intruder's unexpected arrival. Damn that stuck lock.

Instincts surging into protective mode, she tugged Chloe close, positioning herself between her child and the man. He didn't look particularly threatening, but there was definitely something dangerous about him.

A quick catalog of his features convinced Brandy she'd seen him before. High forehead, big brain. *Smart.* Strong jaw, not too square. *Stubborn.* Black eyes, prominent cheekbones and sleek, dark hair. *Sexy.* Lips that were full and firm. *Sensual.* Too bad they were set in such a humorless line.

"I want to see Fenton Futterman."

His voice washed over her like a warm tide. He sounded just like the Midnight Man. No. She *had* heard his voice before, but not in her dreams. He was Stetson, the man she'd run into this afternoon. That explained the haven't-we-met-before vibe. He'd ditched the hat and the sunglasses, changed clothes. He looked different, but the pay-attention voice was unmistakable. Four run-ins in one day. Her universal conspiracy theory took on new meaning, but he was no fantasy man come to life.

"Well? How about it?" he prompted impatiently. His voice was deep, his words packed with authority. He was obviously accustomed to getting what he wanted. Did he expect the attorney in question to appear in a blinding cloud of pixie dust because he so commanded?

"I'm sorry. Mr. Futterman's gone home for the day. You'll have to come back tomorrow. I suggest you make an appointment first. He's a very busy man."

"Yeah, I'll just bet he is. Busy filing nuisance suits. Wait a minute." His dark eyes narrowed, and his penetrating gaze seemed to really see her for the first time. "I know you."

She felt the same way but wouldn't admit the déjà vu he provoked. "Hardly."

He stalked into the office, and his uninvited and overly masculine presence dominated the room. All Brandy knew about him was that he worked for Hotspur. He probably wasn't a threat, but as he loomed between her and the door, something about him set off a shrieking alarm in her brain.

"Cripes, lady." He reached out and ran a brown finger along her cheek. "What's on your face this time?"

Just as it had this afternoon, his touch incited a breathless, dizzy, queasy feeling. She hadn't experienced that combination of sensations since being struck in the stomach by a stray softball in junior high.

"What?" She stepped back, her hand clamping to her cheek where she encountered sticky residue. Branded by the ketchup-soaked French fry she'd snapped out of Chloe's fingers. She wouldn't act as embarrassed as she felt. "I appreciate the gesture, but really, you don't have to follow me around to wipe my face."

"Yeah, well apparently somebody needs to." This time he removed a clean white handkerchief from the back pocket of his dark jeans and scrubbed the smear from her cheek. The handkerchief was warm from being pressed next to his hip, but that didn't explain why her skin flamed in response.

Another unnerving reaction smacked her in the gut, and Brandy backed up again. Chloe slipped around her. The little girl stood in front of the man and looked up, hands planted firmly on her tiny hips.

"Celestian left the door open for you. He said you'd come, but I didn't believe him. You're tall."

"Yeah? Well, you're not." Stetson looked down at Chloe, and his expression softened. Slightly. He had an intriguing face, full of planes and angles. Rugged. Handsome. Brandy shook the thought from her

49

head. What was wrong with her? She never drooled over men.

"I'm five." Chloe believed in sharing important information.

"Congratulations." He turned back to Brandy. "Are you Ulbright?"

"No. My name is Brandy Mitchum. I'm a paralegal here."

"You have my sincere condolences. So Futterman's really not here?" He glanced around, his heavy dark brows drawn down in suspicion. Did he think her employer might be hiding under the desk?

Chloe answered. "Nope. Just us three."

"Three?" The man scowled in Brandy's direction. Scowling seemed to be a habit with him.

"Two. There're only two of us here." Brandy regretted the words as soon as they popped out of her mouth. She was a lousy bluffer. She brandished her cell phone. "But I have 9-1-1 on speed dial. So don't get any ideas."

The incredulous expression on his face told her that getting "ideas" about her was the last thing on his mind. "Why were you out on the road today?"

She bristled at his tone. "Considering how it's a free country *and* a public roadway, I don't have to answer that question. But since you asked so nicely, I was doing my job."

"Your job? Right. Harry Peet." He practically spat out the name. "And what the hell were you thinking leaving the front door unlocked? Any nut job off the street could have wandered in here."

"Yeah, I think one did. What I do is none of your business, but I thought the door *was* locked. And I'll thank you not to swear in front of my child."

"What? Oh. Sorry, kid." Though it seemed genuine, he had trouble coughing up an apology. Either he never made mistakes, or he didn't admit them. He turned his attention back to Brandy. "Are you always that careless?"

"I beg your pardon?" A total stranger was criticizing her? She was no longer afraid of the man, but she was acutely aware of him. He watched her with the same brooding intensity she'd noted earlier today. Which alone would be enough to sap any woman's strength. Teamed with a magnetic physical presence only fully appreciated in close quarters, resistance didn't stand a chance. The gut-level reaction he aroused in her was appalling. She had to hang on to what little annoyance she could.

"All I'm saying, lady, is you need to be more careful. It's dangerous out there. Is this your kid?"

"Yep. I'm Chloe."

"Uh-huh." His lips pulled into what might have been a faint smile. Or a grimace. On him, it was hard to tell.

"Since you're obviously not here to rob the place, what *do* you want?" Brandy relaxed a little, but not much. The verdict was still out on this good-looking, gimme-a-nail-and-I'll-chew-it guy.

Dressed in snug black jeans, white shirt and scuffed cowboy boots, he was a rugged poster boy for testosterone therapy. Maybe he wasn't a thief or mugger, but he'd stolen her breath away. She'd led a nunlike existence since her divorce and was easy prey. Clearly her sheltered hormones revolted against all logic. Nothing else would explain her attraction to this bad-tempered stranger.

On second thought, maybe attraction wasn't what unnerved her. It had to be that nagging sense of recognition, which had nothing to do with their brief encounter on the road today. This stranger tripped switches she had forgotten she possessed. Why did she feel like she'd seen herself reflected in his night-dark eyes many times?

Had their paths crossed long before today?

Ridiculous. If she'd ever met this imposing specimen of male authority, she would remember. Maybe he seemed familiar because once upon a lonely night, she'd glimpsed him in a dream. Was he the Midnight Man?

No, he might look like a dream, but this guy could be a nightmare for all she knew. Since her divorce, she'd formed a clear notion of her ideal man and this dangerous, too-handsome-for-his-own-good hunk was not it. Next time around, she was voting for quiet, stable and unexciting. Safe.

He extended his hand, which was as large and tan as the rest of him. "I didn't mean to frighten you, ma'am. I'm Patrick Templeton."

"Trick!" Chloe chirped.

He frowned again, but managed not to scowl in her innocent, upturned face. "Yeah, that's right. People call me Trick. How did you know?"

Chloe smiled in the direction of the file cabinet. "I'm a good guesser."

The name finally registered with Brandy. "*You're* Patrick Templeton? The owner of Hotspur Well Control?"

"Yeah. I'm also the defendant in Futterman's latest bogus lawsuit." He leaned forward, bracing one hand on the desk beside her hip. His face was too close. She edged back and drew a deep breath, but still couldn't breathe properly. Was he sucking all the oxygen out of the room?

"I don't have time for this, lady," he said in a measured tone. "I have fires to put out."

Brandy couldn't respond for a moment. She was busy fighting an internal wildfire ignited by the disconcerting knowledge that she already knew how kissing him would feel. Impossible. She did not possess that much imagination. Awareness and longing coursed through her like a river of molten gold. What was happening here? Was this what hypnosis was all about?

Finally Chloe tugged on her hand. "Mommy? Trick is talking to you."

"Sorry." She marshaled enough energy to step away from him. She was losing her grip. Fantasy men did not come to life and storm into one's office. She was the one who needed lessons on what was real and what was make-believe. "You have fires to control, and I have bedtime stories to read. Maybe we should call it a night."

"Harry Peet's got everything all wrong," he insisted. "I need —"

"I'm sure you understand why I can't

discuss a pending case with a defendant. If you'd like to make an appointment with Mr. Futterman, call his secretary tomorrow during regular office hours. Now, if you'll excuse us, we were just leaving."

"Right." He seemed confused by her dismissal. Had he never had a request denied before? "Can I help you carry anything?"

Too late to go gallant on her. "No, thank you. I'm quite used to carrying my own load." At the last moment, she remembered the conference documents stacked in the printer tray. She quickly divided the two copies, placed one on her desk and took Chloe with her to drop the other on Futterman's desk where he would find it first thing in the morning.

She expected Templeton to be gone when she returned, but no such luck. "Allow me to show you out."

Apparently no one could show him anything. He led the way to the front door and stood on the sidewalk while Brandy locked the door. The lock didn't stick or fight back this time. Strange. The shiny white pickup with the flaming Hotspur logo on the door was angled into the space next to her battered Ford Escort. The truck's impressive automotive good looks were as intimidating to the little car as its owner's were to her. She tossed her brief-case and purse on the front seat and leaned in the back to buckle Chloe into her booster seat.

"Wait!" Chloe yelled when she started to close the door.

"What, honey?"

"Let Celestian get in first. You don't want to squash him."

"No, I don't." Brandy paused to give Chloe's invisible playmate time to make himself comfortable on the seat. She caught Trick Templeton's amused look. A slow smile transformed his features, making him seem even more familiar.

"Don't ask." She cranked the window down halfway and shut the door.

He backed up, his hands in front of him. "I wasn't about to."

"Mommy, I didn't say goodbye to Trick."

Brandy sighed. Why did her daughter insist on treating this soon-to-be-sued defendant like a long-lost uncle?

"Tell her goodbye," she said, "or we'll be here all night."

"Yes, ma'am." He braced one hand on the car's roof and leaned down to look inside. "Goodbye, Little Bit."

"Don't leave yet, Trick," Chloe whispered.

"Why not?" he whispered back.

"We might need your help."

"Chloe, say goodbye to Mr. Templeton."

"Bye, Trick." She extended her little fingers like a miniature queen deigning to accept a subject's kiss. He reached in, his large hand swallowing hers, and pumped a couple of times.

"Nice meeting you, kid."

"Don't leave yet," Chloe warned again.

"I won't." He walked around the car as Brandy slid behind the steering wheel. "How old is she again?"

"Five."

"Funny. I would've guessed thirty."

"I know." Brandy grinned. "Be sure to call for an appointment tomorrow."

"Don't worry, I will. And I'm sorry if I . . ." His sentence dribbled off.

"Stormed into my office like a renegade SWAT team door kicker and scared the bejeezus out of me and my innocent child?"

"Little Bit didn't seem scared," he pointed out.

"I know. She's more trusting than me."

"Well, I'm sorry. I'm not usually so . . ."

"Demanding?" she supplied cheerfully.

"No, I'm usually demanding. I was going to say rude." He stood beside the little car, backlit by a street lamp's light, which cast soft, familiar shadows across his face. His white shirt practically glowed in the dark. Barely controlled energy hummed around him like a powerful unseen electromagnetic field.

"Apology accepted." She turned the key in the ignition and nothing happened. She tried again with the same frustrating result. She bit back a few colorful curses she couldn't say in front of Chloe. Thanks a bunch, St. Combustion. *For nothing.*

"Is the car dead, Mommy?"

"As the proverbial doornail." Brandy leaned forward and rested her head on the steering wheel. Would this horrible day never end?

"What's a purveeal doornail?" Chloe loved learning new words.

Trick Templeton interrupted before Brandy could answer. "I think I told you to have the engine checked."

"That's right, you did." Brandy sat up and smacked her forehead in mock wonder. "I don't know why I didn't heed your unsolicited, but clearly valuable advice. I could have squeezed in a complete engine diagnostic on one of my many leisurely breaks this afternoon! My mistake!"

"Hey, you don't have to get huffy."

"Huffy does not begin to describe how I am about to get." If she wasn't careful, she might even cry. It was past Chloe's bedtime. She was tired. She'd had a trying day. Tomorrow, she'd have to get up and jump through the hoops again. Figure out how to get the stupid car fixed. Pay the bills. Be a good mom. Do a good job. She might be used to carrying her own load, but life would be a lot easier if she could share the burden.

"How will we get home, Mommy?"

"I don't know yet." If they camped out in her office, she wouldn't be late for work in the morning. That should make Mr. Futterman happy.

Trick Templeton squatted down beside the open window. "Want me to take a look? I'm pretty good with my hands."

"I'll bet you are," she muttered. She didn't dare linger on that thought.

"Look lady, do you want me to look under your hood or not?"

"Sure. Why not? Knock yourself out, cowboy." She reached down and popped the release lever. Trick walked around to the front of the car, raised the hood and ducked under it.

"Trick will fix the battery, Mommy." Where did Chloe get her optimism? Better yet, where did she get her mechanical knowledge?

"I hope so." Brandy let her head drop back against the headrest and closed her eyes. For the first time in her life, she hoped the man poking around under her hood not only had good hands, but fast ones.

Chapter Three

Trick retrieved his toolbox from the truck. Aiming a flashlight into the car's greasy innards, he immediately discovered the problem. After making a few quick adjustments, he leaned around the car's raised hood. "Try it again!"

She turned the key in the ignition, and the ancient engine hiccuped to life. Some engines purred like contented kittens; this one chugged like a rusty lawnmower. That had been left out in the rain. Trick lowered the hood and walked around to the driver's side window, pulling his handkerchief from his back pocket to wipe his hands. Seeing the ketchup stain sent a riveting surge of emotion spiraling through him. He'd experienced a similar reaction when he'd touched Brandy's cheek. Twice.

He had no idea where the unnerving sensations came from or what they meant in the grand scheme of things. Sorting out emotions was complicated. Owning up to them was messier than the gunk on his handkerchief. Time-consuming. Denying

emotions was easy for a man who preferred to keep life neat and simple.

"That should do it." He stood by the car.
An elusive scent made him draw in a deep
breath. Cinnamon. Reminded him of
something, but before he could figure out
what, he noted Brandy's relieved sigh.
Complacency was dangerous, so he added,
"For the moment."

"Mind if I ask what kind of voodoo
magic brought my zombie car back to
life?" She gazed up at him, her face pale in
the street lamp's hazy glow. He'd seen her
in broad daylight and knew the pallor was
artificial. Her smooth skin was warm and
golden. Now that she was off the defen-
sive, she was neither coy nor seductive.
Her delicate features were arresting in
their openness.

*A man would always know where he stood
with her.*

He shrugged off the uncomfortable
thought. Didn't even feel like one of his.
"No magic required. The battery cables
were loose on the terminals. Easily fixed.
All I had to do was tighten them."

She smiled, and he noticed the indenta-
tion of a tiny dimple at the left corner of
her mouth. Long strands of hair had
slipped from an elaborate braid and flut-

tered in the evening breeze like shiny coffee-colored ribbons. Unlike other pretty women, she seemed unaware of her wholesome appeal. Her name suited her. Like the liqueur, her intrinsic sweetness carried a surprising kick. A man with a weakness for her type would find Brandy Mitchum's cheeky charm downright intoxicating.

"The cables were loose?" Her dark brows fretted together. "How could that happen?"

"I don't know," he admitted. "All kinds of things go wrong with old cars."

In the back seat, the little girl clapped a hand over her mouth and giggled.

"Maybe bouncing over those washboard roads today disconnected them," suggested Brandy.

"Maybe." Her theory was as good as any. "An old car is a disaster waiting to happen. You should have gotten —"

"I know. The engine tuned." She held up a hand tipped with bare nails that had probably never had a professional manicure and ticked off the obvious. "The timing adjusted. The brake pads replaced. The leak in the air conditioner line repaired. A new muffler. And oh, how about some new tires while we're dreaming?"

"That would get you started," he conceded, "if you don't mind pouring money down a rat hole."

"I'm well aware of my vehicular shortcomings. Unfortunately I've been a little checkbook-challenged since the move."

"You're new to Odessa?"

"We've been here a little over a month."

"We?" Without thinking, he checked the hand resting on the steering wheel. No wedding ring.

If she noticed, she didn't let on. "Chloe and I. I'm divorced."

"Ah." Why was he glad to hear that? Her marital status was irrelevant. Despite the physical reaction that had gut-punched him when he touched her, Brandy Mitchum was not the kind of woman he got involved with. He knew females, and experience told him this one would expect a lot from a man. Like commitment. She should have a big ornate C tattooed on her forehead to warn guys who didn't possess reliable radar.

Her lack of flirtation is intriguing. Maybe, but only a fool would rise to that challenge. *She'll demand fidelity and promises.* Exactly. He didn't make promises he couldn't keep. His word was his bond. That's how he'd gotten where he was. At thirty-seven, he'd maintained his bachelor status by not getting involved with women who wanted more than he was willing to offer.

Which is damned little these days.

Yeah, but who's keeping score?

Brandy was a mother. Heavily invested in family values. Divorced and unwilling to accept less than her due. No doubt on the prowl for a replacement man. If she hadn't already staked her claim on a neat little house on a quiet little street with lots of pretty little flowers in the yard and a fluffy puppy for the kid, then she was prospecting for one. He'd met — and run from — women like her before. They needed too much. Loose battery cables today, drippy faucets tomorrow. They were highly skilled at sucking a man into the black hole of domesticity.

The take-over started innocently enough. A little project here. Another there. Hang a curtain rod. Rewire a lamp. Then boom. Before God could get the news, a guy was mucking out gutters and cooking burgers on a backyard grill. His time was no longer his own, and all furloughs from the picket fence prison were carefully monitored by the cookie-baking warden. He shuddered at the thought of being locked in for life with no chance of parole.

No way and no thank you. His risk-taking, nomadic lifestyle didn't mix with family duty. All his time and all his energy was devoted to his demanding job. Job? Who was he kidding? Controlling oil well fires was more of a calling. There were easier ways to make a living. Safer ways, too.

He'd ducked the big C by avoiding complicated relationships and choosing women with no apron strings or expectations. Women whose desires were easily satisfied in the bedroom. His plan had worked so far, so why change a winning play?

And who the hell was he arguing with?

"So you have family here?" He wasn't sure why he was stalling. He should climb into the truck right now and get the heck out of Dodge.

"No. Just the two of us."

Did she have to make her situation sound so pitiful? Little mama and forty-pound kid against the world. Good thing he wasn't in the damsel-saving business. Trick took a step back, equating physical distance with the emotional variety.

"My daddy's a sheriff." The little girl piped up from the back seat. "He has a badge and everything."

"He does, huh?" Chloe the Uncanny was another complication. Like their mothers,

66

kids needed things too. Time, attention, nurturing. He wasn't bent that way.

Freedom topped the list of his prized possessions. He could pack a bag and leave at a moment's notice without having to clear his departure with ground control. Exactly the way he liked things. The key to life was traveling light. No strings, no ties and no entanglements. A family would only slow the rocket of his life.

What? You want to die alone? Never knowing real love.

He was happy with the way things were. He didn't need the ballast of stability and love.

"Yep, her daddy's a sheriff, all right." Brandy gave off vibes of calm determination and seemed unaware of Trick's internal power struggle. She smiled again, flashing the dimple. "Duly elected by the citizens of Slapdown, Texas."

Sexy in a nonsexual way, Ms. Earnest Working Mom was definitely not his type. Her beat-all kid compounded the problem. Trick couldn't relate to humans that small or that smart. He didn't understand children any better now than he had when he'd been one himself, an only child because his parents had feared unleashing another fearless dynamo on the world.

His father had chased oil wells around the world, and his mother had followed, leaving Trick with his widowed grandmother on a farm in the Missouri Ozarks. Granny Bett's place had been a growing boy's paradise. Caves to explore, trees to climb, rivers to swim. He'd been as happy as a left-behind child could be, but had joined the family business the second he was old enough to impose his formidable will.

"What?" Brandy frowned. "You're looking at me funny. Do I have something on my face again?"

"No." He'd been lost in a maze of memories. This woman was the worst kind of dangerous. Just being near her conjured up thoughts of hearth and home. Longing for family. "I'm sorry. I know we haven't met before today, but there's something about you that's . . ."

"Familiar?"

"Very."

"How strange," she said. "I was thinking the same thing about you. I'm sure we've seen each other around town."

"That's probably it."

"Mommy? Can Trick come to our house?"

"No, honey. It's getting late, and I'm

sure he has other things to do."

"How about tomorrow?"

The kid was persistent; he'd give her that.

"Can Trick eat with us?" Chloe asked.

"No."

"Well, can he visit?"

"I don't think so." As tired as she had to be, Brandy was patient with her daughter's wheedling questions.

"I want to show him my princess books."

He leaned down and peered into the back seat. "Sorry, Little Bit. I have to work."

"Putting out fires." Little Chloe was as sharp as a brier. He'd only mentioned firefighting in passing.

"That's right. Oil well fires." He gazed into Chloe's wide, dark, knowing eyes, and the door of his heart creaked open against his will, welcoming her to step inside. Scaring the heck out of him.

"Still slaying dragons, Trick?"

He took an involuntary step back. "What?" The child's innocent question prickled the skin on the back of his neck. Despite the evening heat, chilly fingers crept up his spine. Who were these people? Being with them felt both normal and extraordinary at the same time.

Still slaying dragons, Trick? He'd heard those words before, asked in the same gentle manner. Hard as he tried, he couldn't remember when. Further proof of how confused and addled the Mitchums made him. "I know you're a good guesser, Chloe, but where did you come up with that?"

"From my princess storybook." Tiny, pearled teeth filled her grin. "The handsome prince always slays the dragon."

"Right." His taut muscles relaxed, and he let out a relieved breath. Man, Little Bit wasn't the only one with too much imagination. He was attaching meaning where there was none.

"What does slay mean?" Chloe asked.

Before he could answer, Brandy looked over her shoulder. "Slay means to amuse, honey, as in ha, ha, that joke really slays me."

"Oh." The little girl frowned. "So princes make dragons laugh?"

"Yes."

"That doesn't make any sense." Chloe slumped in her booster seat to ponder the comedian prince puzzle.

"Thank you, Mr. Templeton." Brandy's brisk tone let him know the conversation was over. A good mother, she obviously didn't want to give her kid nightmares about mythical creatures being run through by princely swords.

The ruse might have worked with an ordinary kid, but Little Bit wouldn't buy it.

"I appreciate you getting the car running," Brandy continued. "But I really need to take Chloe home to bed."

The innocent statement should not have conjured up images of getting *her* into *his* bed. But it did.

Get your mind out of the gutter. The value of a good woman goes far beyond physical pleasure.

Never mind where it came from, the suggestion had merit. Nice little mamas weren't into casual what's-in-it-for-me sex, and that's all he had time for these days. And on the fly, at that. He'd better cut and run. Brandy was as tempting as her name, but she was a hair-trigger trap waiting to spring.

He drove the conversation down a safer road. "You'll keep having mechanical problems. Take my advice and trade this heap in on something more reliable."

"Right. I'll add 'new car' to my wish list. Item number 4,783." Her weary tone softened the sarcasm, but he couldn't help wondering what the other four thousand plus wished-for items included.

71

A woman alone, working long hours to support a child, didn't have an easy life. *She wasn't kidding when she said she was used to carrying her own load.* Yeah, too bad she had to bear so much on her delicate shoulders. Another unbidden thought seized him. *Might be satisfying to ease her burden in some way.*

"Good night, Mr. Templeton." Brandy shifted the transmission into Reverse.

"Call me Trick." He should let her go before he got into any more trouble.

She shook her head. "I shouldn't be on a first-name basis with one of my employer's defendants. Not ethical."

"I see." He'd been so distracted by the woman's disarming dimple and darling daughter that he'd almost forgotten she worked for the law firm suing him on behalf of that idiot Harry Peet. Yet another reason not to get involved.

There was a lot at stake in this lawsuit, and she was the enemy. They couldn't fraternize. Hell, they shouldn't even be talking.

"Good night, Ms. Mitchum." Then as she drove away, he murmured, "I'll see you in court."

"Isn't Trick nice, Mommy? You do think Trick is nice, don't you?" Due to the late

72

hour, Chloe had skipped her nightly bath. With face washed and teeth brushed, she'd slipped into Powerpuff Girl pajamas before climbing into bed.

"I suppose so." "Nice" was hardly the word Brandy would choose to describe Trick Templeton. Her daughter had great language skills, but her vocabulary did not include words like mesmerizing and intimidating.

"Can I have a story?"

"Not tonight, baby. Give Mommy a kiss and get to sleep."

After they exchanged a noisy smooch, Brandy pressed a gentle kiss in the center of Chloe's palm and folded her fingers over it. The spare kiss was a long-standing tradition they shared, because one wasn't enough to last through the night. Brandy shivered at the thought of the Midnight Man's next visit. Would this be the night he got close enough to kiss?

Chloe climbed over the covers to the end of the bed, smacked the air and bounced back to snuggle under the flower-sprigged comforter.

"What was that all about?"

"I had to give Celestian a kiss, too."

"Oh. Right." Him, again. Still unsure how to handle the situation, Brandy smoothed the covers over Chloe and stroked damp blond hair from her face. "I guess it's fun to have an invisible friend."

"Most of the time," Chloe corrected.

"Just so you realize he's not real."

"But he *is* real, Mommy." Chloe grinned as her gaze tracked movement from the bed to the other side of the room.

"In here, sure." Brandy gently tapped her temple. "He only lives in your imagination."

"Nope. He's right over there." Chloe pulled her arm from under the pink sheet and pointed. "He's sitting on the toy box now. He's happy 'cause Trick came tonight. He said he would, but I wasn't so sure."

Brandy frowned. This had been a long day, full of strange encounters. Not only was she too tired to deal effectively with this troubling problem, she wasn't sure what course of action would speed the pretend friend along its natural course. It didn't seem right to impose her will and insist Chloe admit Celestian wasn't real. What was the harm in indulging her child's innocent fantasies a little longer? It was her own fantasies she should be worried about.

Far more disturbing than the new playmate, was her daughter's unlikely fascination with Trick Templeton. She'd never taken to a strange man the way she'd taken to him. The fact that she'd incorporated Templeton into the fantasy by having Celestian "talk" about him was especially troublesome.

Okay, Trick was definitely fantasy material, but not for a five-year-old. Celestian was to blame for encouraging Chloe's interest in a man she would never see again.

Brandy sighed. Celestian wasn't real. She couldn't blame him for anything.

"Good night, honey." Shaking the muddled thoughts from her head — Lord, she was exhausted — Brandy switched on the Pooh Bear nightlight and trudged to the door.

"Aren't you going to tell Celestian good night too?"

She'd play the game. For now. "Good night, Celestian."

"He says 'fare thee well.' Isn't that funny?"

"Very."

"Celestian says we did good today. Do you think we did good, Mommy?"

"What do you mean?" She paused at the doorway, leaning wearily against the frame. She *was* tired. In body and spirit. And she was tired of hearing about Celestian and Trick Templeton. She needed to rest. As titillating as her dreams could be, she hoped the Midnight Man would not show up tonight.

"Do you think we did good with Trick?" Chloe repeated.

"I don't know." That wasn't true. She was pretty sure she hadn't done well with Trick at all. While she'd been as shocked as a bug in a zapper when they touched, he had not seemed impressed. And why should he be? With his face and body and money, Templeton probably had to beat supermodels off with a stick. He wouldn't look twice at a divorcée with a pile of debts taller than her kid.

Despite her determination to be independent, she'd been thinking lately how nice it would be to have someone to share her life with. Someone willing to take on part of the load she was destined to carry. A partner. A full-time stepfather for Chloe who wouldn't grumble about driving the carpool. Trick Templeton, with his imposing good looks, gruff personality and fast-lane life, did not fit the daydream.

So what was his connection to those sensual dreams she'd been having? Her face tingled at the memory of his warm fingers gently stroking her cheek through soft cotton. She shook her head again. Enough of that.

"Sleep tight, sweetie. Morning comes early." Thank goodness tomorrow was Friday. Brandy needed the weekend to recover from today's excitement.

"Don't forget to set the alarm." Chloe flopped over on her side and tucked her hands under her cheek.

"I won't." Brandy left the door open a crack. Whenever she got discouraged and wondered why she kept running the maze, all she had to do was look at Chloe. Her daughter was her reward for doing something right. Chloe kept her grounded and gave her a reason to live. Things were hard now, but they would get better.

After a few months, she'd be eligible for a raise. If she continued to do a good job, Futterman would have to increase her salary. With the extra income, she could get ahead on her bills and maybe sock some away in savings. Independence had been a long time coming, but the security she'd longed for all her life was finally within her reach.

Hindered by the clumsiness of fatigue, she got ready for bed, too. She switched on the bedside lamp and opened the library book she'd been reading. After a few minutes, she gave up and set the bestseller aside. The words on the page couldn't engage her interest. Not when her mind insisted on replaying every detail of her meeting with Trick Templeton. She closed her eyes but could still see his face.

Why was he haunting her?

I know you, he'd said earlier in her office. She buried her head under her pillow but could still hear his voice.

Why did he sound like the echo of a dream?

The next morning, Trick headed downtown. He made sure his crews were on the job before carving out time to deal with that ridiculous lawsuit. Wasting valuable firefighting time on stupid, frivolous litigation put him in a sour mood. Didn't he have enough on his mind without this aggravation? The Hotspur office had fallen into chaos in the two weeks since office manager Wylodene Talbott had jumped ship. Ace was answering phones and taking messages, but the old coot didn't know a thing about bookkeeping.

Reliable, hardworking Wylodene had been a fixture at Hotspur as long as Trick could remember. He'd never had to think about the clerical side of the business, much less worry about it, because steady Wylodene had taken care of everything. Then she'd met some aging Don Juan at a senior citizen square dance and the next thing Trick knew, the two had eloped to Vegas. Married by an Elvis impersonator. Who knew the quiet little sixty-year-old had that much romance left in her?

Romance. Bah, humbug!

Not only did he have professional problems to deal with, he suddenly had a personal one. He never had personal problems because he lived his life in a way that precluded them. So why was he losing sleep and concentration over Brandy Mitchum? Even if she did work for the lawyer who was suing him, he'd probably never see her again except in a court of law.

No sooner had the thought formed in his mind than he pulled into the stream of traffic and found himself following a beat-up purple Ford. There couldn't be more than one of those things on the road.

Coincidence was getting out of control. He couldn't take his eyes off the driver's fancy braid. Brandy. He'd spent a restless night trying not to think about her and here she was. Again. The turn signal came on, and the little car rumbled down a side street. Trick drove on, suppressing a powerful urge to follow, just so he could see that danged dimple again.

Unable to meet with the suddenly inaccessible but eternally annoying Fenton Futterman, Trick stopped in to talk to his own attorney. He didn't like what Charles Thorson had to say.

"No way in hell!" For emphasis, Trick banged his fist down hard on his long-time legal counsel's polished desk. "I am not giving in to that fruitcake."

Charles leaned back in his chair. "As your friend *and* your lawyer, Trick, I advise you to settle the suit out of court."

"Why? He doesn't have a case."

"Going to court is an iffy thing. You never know how a jury will rule. I've seen plaintiffs win decisions with less than nothing going for them. A case like this is all about emotions. If they feel sorry for Harry Peet or perceive him as the underdog, they could find in his favor despite the lack of evidence against Hotspur."

"Well, that's comforting to know." Trick couldn't conceal his bitterness. Thanks to Brandy Mitchum, he hadn't slept well last night. He was running on the high-octane rocket fuel Ace Munro fobbed off as coffee. Ace had taken over brewing duties since Wylodene's defection.

"Some juries develop an attitude of 'let the big corporation cover the little guy. They can afford to pay.' I'm not saying that's fair, but it happens."

"Now there's a scorching indictment of the legal system in this country, if I ever heard one."

Charles shrugged. "I know. But you pay me a sizeable retainer to give you my best legal advice, so here it is in a pecan shell: settle."

"I'm not paying Harry Peet $90,000. His whole frigging operation isn't worth that much, lock, stock and milk buckets."

"He'll take less."

"I can't believe he's claiming loss of income and mental distress due to aggravation. What about my aggravation? I have better things to do than mess around with a baseless lawsuit. He thinks the noise from my firefighting equipment disturbed his cows? Gimme ten minutes alone with the guy, and I'll show him a disturbance."

"Calm down, buddy."

"Calm down? I come back from Washington and a meeting with the Department of Defense to present a contingency plan for fighting oil well fires in the Middle East and get slapped with a summons because some nutcase says I'm harassing his damn cows. Cows! You don't know me very well if you think I'll roll over and take this."

Charles shuffled a stack of legal documents. "According to Futterman's suit, the Milk of Human Kindness Dairy's success depends on the contentment of his cows."

"You were kidding when you said he plays Chopin in the milking barn, right?" Trick asked.

"No. That part is true. He says music decreases the animals' stress."

Trick hooted. "Stress? Now I've heard everything."

"The milk is wholesome and natural because . . ." Charles paused, thumbing through the papers until he found the phrase he was looking for. "Peet's cows are, quote, delicate in their bovine sensibilities. Unquote."

Trick smacked a fist into his palm and spoke in a measured tone. "Cows do not have sensibilities. Hell, cows don't even have sense! They're as dumb as sacks of sand."

"I agree." Charles sighed. "But he claims the herd was so upset by the constant stream of equipment, trucks and men to the fire site that milk production was affected. As a result, he couldn't meet his contract with the grocery chain, and they found another supplier which put a crimp in his cash flow."

"Yeah, well, I'd like to put a crimp in something else," Trick muttered.

"Let's not resort to violence. We have other options."

"Peet never should have babied his damn cows with Chopin in the first place. What else does he do? Provide them with aromatherapy and reflexology?"

Charles smiled. "Those details aren't mentioned in the complaint."

"I'm not paying."

"You might want to reconsider. This is obviously a nuisance suit, but in the long run settling will be a lot cheaper and easier than taking the time and trouble to fight it out in court. Trust me. Just throw the guy a bone and get back to the important things. Like saving wells so the oil companies can keep down the cost of gasoline for my SUV."

"Whoa! Back up." Trick braced his hands on the lawyer's desk and leaned forward. "What did you just say again?"

"Fighting the suit isn't worth the paperwork and you should offer him less."

"After that. About the cost of gasoline."

"Have you been to the pumps lately?"

"Yeah." Trick's face split in a wide grin.

"And so has every potential juror in west Texas. This is the Permian Basin, the heart of petroleum country. Odessa is one of the major oil field technology centers in the world."

"Yeah, so?"

"Don't you see? How is Futterman going to find twelve of my peers who don't have a stake in the oil business?"

Charles took only a moment to catch up. "Oh, yeah, I see where you're headed."

"Peet's not exactly a sympathetic figure. Maybe in California among the tree huggers and spotted owl folks, but not here. In Texas, we like good old boys in boots better than we like middle-aged hippies with ponytails."

Charles slapped Trick's back. "That comment isn't exactly politically correct, but I think you've just defined our defense."

"So you're game?"

Charles grinned and an evil glint touched his eyes. "Oh, I'm game all right. Fighting is going to be time-consuming and expensive, but if we win, they have to pay the court costs."

"Serves them right for their 'get something for nothing' attitude." Trick relaxed. He felt better than he had since being served the summons. He'd taken Brandy's advice and called Futterman's office to make an appointment. The secretary said her boss was busy and would only talk to Hotspur's legal counsel. Too bad. The shyster should have played the game, because now he was in for a round of hardball.

Obviously delighted by the prospect of trouncing his obnoxious colleague, Charles rubbed his hands together in exaggerated glee. "I'm actually looking forward to hauling Fenton Let-Me-Be-Your-Legal-Voice Futterman into court. He's a trial-shy blowhard. He picks wealthy defendants who are too busy to fight and whose legal departments advise them to make him go away by paying through the nose."

Trick sat down. "My nose has been a little out of joint lately, so that route is out of the question." He wasn't sure why he felt so antsy. Sitting still was an effort. Concentrating impossible.

Charles leaned back in his chair. "This could be the most fun I've had in a long time, buddy."

"So you're willing to give Futterman his day in court?"

"I can't wait. At the risk of sounding self-interested, winning won't hurt my reputation any."

"Regardless of who wins, there's principle at stake." Trick knew the jury might not see things his way, but he wouldn't go down without a fight. "Right is right and wrong is wrong. Hotspur was doing the right thing by capping that blowout. Peet's wrong to make us look like the villains of the piece and trying to capitalize on our efforts."

"Juries are peculiar critters. This may not be a cut-and-dried case," Charles warned.

"It is to me. Besides, I'm feeling a little confrontational and would like nothing better than to kick some dairy fairy butt in court." That would put him and Brandy on opposite sides of the issue, but just as well. He needed to stop thinking about her and get back to business.

"If it weren't nine in the morning," Charles said with uncommon cheer, "we could celebrate with brandy."

"Brandy? What the hell's that supposed to mean?" The name filled Trick with alarm. The woman had taken up residence in his thoughts, filling his mind with strange ideas. Was Charles in on the conspiracy to drive him nuts?

"You know, a toast?" The lawyer lifted his arm in the requisite gesture.

"Right. A toast. No need." Trick ignored the tension ratcheting his nerves up into the red zone. Runaway imagination was as dangerous as a stray spark. "The thought of winning is intoxicating enough."

"So you're not afraid to fight this out?" Charles pulled a legal pad from a drawer and began taking notes.

"Afraid?" Trick settled back in his chair and rested a booted foot on the opposite knee. "I battle hell-breathing fire for a living. Do you think a pansy ambulance chaser like Fenton Futterman scares me?" Even if his legal assistant did. Just a little.

"Nothing scares you, pal. Ready for battle?"

Trick narrowed his eyes, firming his resolve. "Let the games begin."

Chapter Four

Brandy didn't have time to think about Trick Templeton or Harry Peet's suit against Hotspur. She spent Friday afternoon on other cases, interviewing a prospective client confined to bed and researching the city's zoning codes at City Hall. Working outside the office pressure cooker was a blessing at times — especially when Mr. Futterman was around. On the downside, legwork put Brandy behind with everything else.

Thanks to hard work, clean living and pure luck, she was ready to call it a week by a quarter past five. The rest of the staff had already started the weekend, but Brandy stayed to clear her desk and prepare a to-do list for Monday morning. She'd just finished listing item number five when Mr. Futterman came in.

Stormed in.

"I want you to know, I looked like a fool in front of Judge Klingman today," he barked without preamble. "What do you have to say about that?"

Brandy didn't know how to respond to the startling announcement. If he wanted confirmation, she would gladly agree. Futterman did indeed look foolish in his dark mob boss suit, rattlesnake cowboy boots and dead-on-the-vine hair plugs. A gleeful tyrant with a pinched face and gaunt frame, he looked like the illicit love child of Jack Sprat and the Queen of Hearts. The grimmest character in Grimm's fairy tales.

"I'm sorry, sir." She slipped the legal pad into a desk drawer and waited to see where the conversation would go.

"You *should* be sorry. Klingman was not amused. Neither was I. How do you expect me to get a judge to sign off on this?" He slammed down the pretrial documents she'd printed out last night. "I demand an explanation."

Shaken by his unreasonable anger, Brandy picked up the papers and flipped through them. Her brows drew together in alarm. The first few pages looked fine, but the rest consisted of nonsense words and cryptic computer symbols. "I don't understand —"

"It's gibberish. Didn't they teach you to proofread at that business school you attended?"

"Of course. The file was fine when I checked it last night. I made two copies." She stepped over to the file cabinet and pulled out the one she'd kept. It was letter perfect. Exactly as it should have been. The copies had printed out at the same time. How could one be right, and the other be so wrong? "Look."

Futterman snatched the file out of her hands, skimmed the contents and flung it down on her desk. "Why didn't you give me this one? I don't appreciate being made to look incompetent."

"I have no idea what happened." On second thought, maybe she did. She'd been worried about Chloe's new imaginary playmate and the strange events of the afternoon. She'd been in a rush to get home. Trick Templeton's unexpected appearance had distracted her further. In her haste to get rid of him, she'd taken shortcuts. Fallen down on the job.

On top of all that, she'd had another disturbing dream last night. Mr. Midnight was getting bolder. Or at least her subconscious was sending her bolder messages. Dreams full of fantasy foreplay didn't exactly make for restful sleep. She'd arrived at work this morning tired and muzzyheaded. She had glanced through her copy of the complaint before filing it but could honestly say she hadn't even given the one she'd placed on Futterman's desk a cursory look. The weight of her boss's displeasure settled in her stomach like a burning stone.

Futterman's irate gaze snagged on the tiny Barbie figurine from Chloe's meal box, and he triumphantly snatched it up like a damning piece of evidence. He tossed it from hand to hand before slamming the toy back on her desk with enough force to make Brandy jump.

"Did you bring your child to the office last night, Ms. Mitchum?"

"Yes, sir, but —"

"Have I not made my feelings clear on that subject?"

"Yes, sir, but —"

"But nothing! I thought you understood. Firm policy prohibits you from mixing your personal life with work."

"Actually, it was the other way around. We were already on our way home when you called. It was late. After hours."

"There are no 'after hours' in this office. If you want to work for me, you must be ready to respond at a moment's notice. What am I paying you for? What's more important? Your job or your personal life?"

Brandy bristled. Wait a doggone minute. This was too much. Futterman-Ulbright wasn't a fire department or an elite military unit defending national security. The firm's goal was profit, not public good. She wasn't a partner. Futterman didn't pay her enough to "respond at a moment's notice." Her current salary was more than she'd ever made before, but it was far less than industry average.

Brandy met her boss's furious gaze with calm and reason. She had made a mistake and would face the music. "I'm sorry you were inconvenienced, Mr. Futterman." She was. "I'm sorry I didn't proofread your copy." She *really* was. "But I won't apologize for taking care of my child. If anything, I should regret letting work take precedence over family time. I'm not making excuses, but this wouldn't have happened if Trick Templeton hadn't come in —"

Futterman stopped his angry little stomp around the office. "Templeton? Patrick Templeton was here last night?"

"Yes. He stopped by to speak to you —"

"What? That puts a whole new spin on things. What did you say to him, Ms. Mitchum?" Futterman's face had gone as pasty as a heart attack victim's. "Did you encourage him to fight Harry Peet's lawsuit against Hotspur?"

So much for calm and logic. She wouldn't fight tantrum with tantrum, but neither would she be falsely accused. "No! Of course not. I did take a legal ethics course at that business school I attended. I don't advise defendants."

She would, however, pay to watch Fenton Futterman cross-examine the magnetic firefighter. She'd like to see how long Rumplestiltskin held up under the scrutiny of Templeton's intimidating scowl. The thought provided an asbestos shield against the blistering heat of Futterman's displeasure. "I told him to call back today and make an appointment to speak to *you*."

"You must have said or done something. Given him the wrong idea. Ticked him off. Pushed his buttons."

"Why do say that?"

"Because he refuses to settle."

"What?" She wasn't really surprised. Templeton didn't seem like the give-in or give-up type.

"You heard me. His attorney called ten minutes ago and said he was moving for a summary judgment."

The implications weren't lost on Brandy.

Unless the case was resolved in mediation, it would most likely go to trial. Futterman's reaction began to make sense. The court system was shifting to a rocket docket, making it tougher for the trial-shy lawyer to avoid the courtroom.

Obviously he was worried. Maybe even nervous. He needed every fee he could collect to support his lavish lifestyle. If Templeton wouldn't pony up, the case would go to court, which was way out of Futterman's comfort zone. Break a leg, boss. She composed her features, careful not to let him know the traitorous direction of her thoughts.

Fenton Futterman had finally met his match.

"If Mr. Peet's case is as strong as you say, there shouldn't be a problem."

"No problem! Of course, there's a problem. And it's your fault." He flapped around the room like an angry crow.

"I take responsibility for the conference documents. I should have checked them more carefully. But I had nothing to do with Templeton's decision."

"I never should have hired you," he muttered. "Why didn't you tell me your husband defeated my son in the sheriff's election a couple of years ago?"

Maybe Futterman was upset about more than the document error. "I didn't mention it because Joe Mitchum is no longer my husband and wasn't at the time of the election. I didn't think my personal life was relevant."

"Obviously it is. This is no job for a single mother."

He put roughly the same spin on the words as he would have put on brain-dead armadillo. Brandy silently counted to five before responding. "You are flirting with discrimination, sir."

"Don't tell me the law, young lady!" he snapped.

She stole a glance at the clock. Quarter to six. Chloe. Time to go. She scooped up her purse and briefcase. "I'm sorry, Mr. Futterman. I promise nothing like this will ever happen again."

"Are you in a hurry, Ms. Mitchum? Are work-related matters keeping you from a pressing social engagement?"

"No, but my daughter's child care program closes at six. I barely have time to get there."

"By all means. Go!" He whirled around and stalked to the door, then turned, a smug look on his face. "In fact, take all the time you need. Since your parental responsibilities make it impossible for you to focus adequate attention on your work, perhaps you should seek a less demanding position."

"I beg your pardon?"

"I don't think this is working out."

"What are you saying?"

"Do I have to spell it out?"

"Considering how confused I am at the moment, yes. Please do." Brandy knew what was coming and this time the déjà vu was understandable. So were the queasy stomach and sweaty palms. She'd gotten the boot before. As much as she dreaded to hear them, he had to say the words. Even if they were the very last words she'd expected to hear today.

"I'll have the bookkeeper put your paycheck and two weeks severance pay in the mail tomorrow."

"I'm sorry" was all she could say. The man's smug satisfaction hit her like a slap. He'd changed her life with no more thought than he would have used to kick a stone out of his path.

This simply could not happen.

And then it did.

"You're fired, Ms. Mitchum!"

That night, Brandy did her weeping after Chloe went to bed. She cried in the dark until she finally fell into a dream that seemed more real than the unbelievable events of the day. Mr. Midnight had sat beside her, quiet and amorphous, not speaking or touching. Just being, filling a void in the night and in her heart. Before, his visits had been distinctly sensual. Not this time. Somehow, without saying the words, he had let her know she was not to blame for losing her job. That she would soon find another one. A better one. Thanks to his comforting presence, she had awakened just before dawn, feeling less alone in the world and more determined to succeed than ever.

Futterman's vindictive dismissal was a punch below the belt, but by Monday morning, she had pulled herself together and was ready to move on. Instead of stewing and fretting about her suddenly jobless state, Brandy considered the setback little more than a speed bump on the freeway of her new life. It might slow her down, but it wouldn't stop her.

Survivors didn't let the grass grow beneath their feet, and Brandy hit the nearest personnel office as soon as she dropped Chloe off at school. Her daughter's smiling, trusting face was the reason she couldn't accept defeat or lapse into depression or become bitter. Unemployment was not the end of the world. Fenton the Fink had declined to give her a recommendation, but she didn't need one. She would find work on her own merits.

Unfortunately Mr. Johnson, the job counselor at Flash Personnel, wasn't very encouraging. "The job market is tight right now. We don't have any paralegal positions on file. As a matter of fact, we don't get many professional listings. Most of those are filled through word of mouth."

"I understand." Brandy's optimism faltered, but didn't fail. She was used to opposition and wouldn't wave a white flag just yet. If she couldn't work in her chosen field, she would do something else. Temporarily.

"Have you tried a professional recruiter?"

She'd hoped that wouldn't be necessary. Professional recruiters charged costly fees. "Not yet."

"Did you apply for state unemployment benefits?"

Unemployment? Her situation wasn't that desperate. Was it? A growing knot of doubt formed in her stomach, making her queasy. She never should have shared the cinnamon toast Chloe had requested for breakfast. "That's not an option. Even if I qualify, I won't get enough to pay my bills and support my daughter. I'm willing to work outside my field, if necessary."

The counselor consulted the form she'd so confidently completed less than ten minutes ago and keyed information into his computer. A list of job openings appeared on the monitor. "Unless you have five years experience as a welder or carry an LPN certification, we don't have anything close to the salary and benefits you require."

She swallowed hard, firming her resolve. She wasn't asking for much. A chance. That was all. "What *do* you have with medical coverage?" She was willing to work hard, for less money, but insurance for Chloe was essential.

Mr. Johnson scrolled through the listings. "Evening attendant at a funeral home?"

"I have a small child and no one to care for her after six." Even if she could find a sitter, she couldn't work the late shift. She didn't spend enough time with Chloe as it was.

He looked up. "I guess night watchman is out too, huh?"

"Afraid so." The man was kind enough to try and relieve her worry with humor. She returned his smile, despite the mounting dread rumbling through her. "I'm willing to compromise." She'd had plenty of experience settling for less.

"Here's an opening for a hospital cafeteria worker. Three twelve-hour shifts Friday through Sunday, minimum wage to start, with a raise in three months."

Frustration edged out despair. "Mr. Johnson, because of my child's school and day care schedule, I need to work eight to five, Monday through Friday. I don't want to be difficult, but I'm the head of the household and a trained professional. I need a decent wage and family medical benefits."

"I understand." He printed a short list of current job openings for her to consider, but dishearteningly, none of them were right. The day jobs available were low-paying file clerk or receptionist positions without ben-efits. Higher-paying jobs required special-ized skills she did not possess. She'd become a paralegal in order to climb the job market ladder, and here she was on the bottom rung again. Right where she'd started.

No. She was worse off than before. She'd spent a lot of time and money acquiring specialized knowledge and had nothing to show for her investment. She might as well have bought a lottery ticket instead.

The counselor suggested she send her résumé to local law firms, but doing so would be futile. Less than a month ago, she'd accepted the only vacant paralegal position in town. Fenton Futterman was supposed to be the solution, but he'd become the problem. She would smile and shake the counselor's hand. Thank him for his help. Then she had to walk out without a job or any hope of one. This wasn't the way things were supposed to go.

Now even her dreams were wrong.

"I'll put you into the system, Ms. Mitchum. Let's hope what you need comes along soon."

What she needed was a miracle. Nothing short of divine intervention would save her now, so she sent up a silent prayer, asked for a sign. Hope was slipping through her fingers, along with independence and self-respect. If she didn't find a job soon, she'd have to give up on her goals. Uproot Chloe again. Move back in with her parents and work in a mini-mart. Be a failure.

Life was hard, but making a living was harder.

She was halfway to the door when she noticed the overpowering scent of cinnamon. It seemed to be everywhere these days. Before she could consider the source, the power went out and plunged the windowless room into darkness. If this was a sign, it was of the ominous variety.

Mr. Johnson groaned. "What now? We're not having a storm, are we?"

"I don't think so. There wasn't a cloud in the sky when I came in." Brandy fumbled for the knob. When she opened the door, light flooded in from the hallway. At the end of the corridor, the reception area was also well lit. In other rooms, people were working at computers or talking to clients. Her scalp prickled. That spooky feeling was becoming way too familiar.

"I wonder what the problem is?" Mr. Johnson asked.

"I don't know. The power failure seems limited to your office."

He laughed. "That's a good excuse to go home early."

Before she could respond, the overhead light flickered on. "Guess not."

"Well now, this is weird." He glanced at the now-bright computer screen, took a closer look and waved her back into the office. "Don't leave, Ms. Mitchum. Come in and sit down."

"What is it?"

"The computer didn't reboot like it usually

does after a brownout. The monitor came on with a new screen displayed. Oddest thing I ever saw. There's a job opening listed now that wasn't there before."

A shiver passed through Brandy. She didn't know prayers could be answered so quickly. Could this be the miracle she'd requested? A cinnamon-scented miracle. She sniffed the air. Someone in the office next door must be having a snack. Apprehensive, but also intrigued, she sank into the chair across from Mr. Johnson's desk. "So what's the job?"

The counselor read the new listing aloud. "Office manager needed to work in demanding setting. Must be calm eye in the middle of storm and able to start immediately. Organizational abilities a must. Applicant should be self-starter and possess excellent computer and communication skills. Forty hours a week, 8:00 a.m. to 5:00 p.m., Monday through Friday. No evenings or weekends required. Full family medical and dental benefits. Paid vacation and sick leave. Starts at $40K per year but salary commensurate with experience."

Mr. Johnson looked up and grinned. "Sounds like a match made in heaven, doesn't it, Ms. Mitchum?"

"Yes. It does. What's the catch? Do I have to relocate to Greenland?"

"Nope. It's local."

He told her the address, and she nearly choked on a gasped breath. "That's three blocks from my house."

"Convenient."

"Yes." Very.

"The position seems custom-made for you. Too good to be true." Mr. Johnson printed the job description and contact information. "I'd call and set up an interview, but it says here no appointment is needed. That's unusual. Maybe you should hustle over there before they hire someone else."

Brandy read the firm's name off the paper he'd given her. This time she did choke. The heaven-sent job wasn't too good to be true.

It was too strange to be real.

A shiver of anticipation rippled through her. This *had* to be a sign. The company needing a new office manager was Hotspur Well Control.

"Where the hell is the Sandco contract?" Trick looked around the messy Hotspur office with distaste. How had things gotten so far out of control in such a short time? He shoved a file drawer shut with enough force to make Ace Munro flinch.

"I dunno, boss. I'm in charge of coffee making and phone answering. Not filing." The grizzled sixty-two-year-old handed Trick a mug of his dangerous brew. "Here, drink some blood pressure medicine before you have a stroke."

Trick accepted the coffee. The grin he flashed his old friend was the only apology needed. Ace had been his father's righthand man, a top-notch firefighter in his day. His day was about over, but nothing short of an act of God would make Ace retire. Since Wylodene's defection two weeks ago, the old man had made himself useful in the office, manning phones and handling dispatch. However, he didn't know squat about computers, nor was he the most organized bean in the pot.

"How could Wylo run off and leave us in a mess like this?" Trick bemoaned.

"Oh, I dunno. Maybe spending her golden years with a man who treats her like the queen of the castle was more appealing than taking grief from you, day in and day out."

"She worked for Hotspur over thirty years!" The savvy little woman was as strong and flexible as the tree that shared her nickname. Like a willow she could bend without breaking and had been a fixture in the office so long, Trick couldn't imagine doing business without her.

"There ya go. You answered your own question." Ace pushed a pile of invoices out of the way and perched on the corner of Wylodene's old desk. "Why don't you just hire someone to replace her?"

"Replace her? How could anyone replace the person who invented the job? Pop brought Wylo on board when he started the business. I can't believe she'd up and abandon me like this."

"Wylodene was your office manager," Ace snorted. "Not your mother. Get over it."

"Maybe she'll come back. Once the honeymoon is over."

Ace laughed. "You don't know much about romance, do you, boy? She's a happily married lady now. With a husband who appreciates her. Come back? Here? Ha! Since Elvis performed the ceremony, we have a better chance of seeing the King of Rock and Roll show up around here than we do her."

"Damn love, anyway." Ace was right. He'd depended on Wylodene, and now she was gone. There was a lesson in there somewhere.

Ace's grin flashed the new teeth that had

set him back a month's pay. "Now that's the attitude of a man who's never experienced the real thing."

Trick didn't have time to debate his love life or lack thereof. He sipped the hot coffee. "So what are we going to do? We're behind on billing. The invoices are piling up. I can't tell accounts payable from accounts receivable. And this is the worst excuse for coffee I've ever tasted!"

"Like it or leave it. Don't make me no difference." Ace stood up and walked to the door. "But since you asked. I've got two little words for ya. Hire a manager."

Trick frowned. "That's three words, you old coot."

Ace just shook his head. "That's what I'm talking about."

"What?"

"Do you have to be such a pain in the butt all the time?"

"I'm not a pain in the butt. Am I?"

"Yeah, you are. Maybe if you'd paid more attention to Wylo, you would have seen her elopement coming."

"She could have warned me."

"Hell, man! She did. You were too busy to notice."

Women and their behavior would always be a mystery to Trick. Maybe he should have tried harder over the years to decipher their female code. "How am I going to replace her?"

Ace shrugged. "Surely in a state as big as Texas, you can find someone who hasn't heard how hard it is to work for you."

After Ace left, Trick continued looking for the Sandco contract. He eventually found it, not in the S file where it should have been, but in the X file. Figured. Returning to his own office, he'd just finished making a phone call when Ace opened the door and stuck his head in.

"Hallelujah, boss. I think our prayers have been answered."

He rocked forward in his chair. "Wylodene's back?"

"Nope. But there's a little lady out front who says she's here to apply for the office manager job. Why didn't you tell me you'd contacted an employment agency?"

"Because I didn't."

"She said Flash Personnel sent her over. I think you oughta talk to her. Looks like the take-charge type to me."

Given everything else he had to worry about, Trick couldn't work up much surprise at the mystery applicant's unexpected arrival. A lot of strange things had happened lately. What was one more? "Fine. Show her in."

He went back to jotting down notes from his phone conversation. The door opened, and the applicant walked in, looking like a dream come true.

Now he was surprised.

Chapter Five

Trick couldn't have been more startled if his visitor *had* been the king of rock and roll stopping by for a chat and a grilled peanut butter and banana sandwich. He hid his reaction behind a practiced poker face. Brandy Mitchum's unexpected appearance in his office made a weird kind of sense. Like fitting a piece into a partially finished jigsaw puzzle without seeing the picture. Blame luck or fate or fortune cookies, but his path had crossed hers frequently the past few days.

She's here for a reason.

And he wanted to find out what that reason was. Brandy stood by the door clutching a large purse. Her big brown eyes were wary, her body poised for flight. A doe weighing her options while facing down a rifle-toting hunter. When had he come to inspire fear in nice women?

Before he could invite her in, the drapes near the window rustled in a stiff breeze, and a distinctive scent wafted in. Cinnamon. Reminded him of the snickerdoodles he'd pilfered from Granny Bett's cookie jar, all those years ago. He hadn't eaten one in ages, so why was he thinking about them now? He glanced at the window. Closed. A draft from the air-conditioning vent must have scattered the stack of papers off his desk. He reached to retrieve them, taking the opportunity to regain his composure before facing the pretty paralegal.

He could have sworn his head bumped something when he bent over, but a second look revealed nothing there to bump.

She belongs here. Can't you see that?

No. He couldn't see that. Nor did he want to. He sat up, straightened the papers and was hit with another freaky sensation. Time had stopped for a moment. Brandy was still standing just as she had been, waiting to be invited in or shooed off. She looked nervous and expectant and not too happy to see him. Funny. He was uncommonly pleased to see her.

Usually when he took pleasure in women, it affected him from the waist down, not the neck up. Normally he'd be speculating about the curves beneath the plain suit and prim blouse. Imagining how her dark mane would look freed from its complicated braid. Loosened and tangled

111

from a passionate turn on his pillow. That was a curiosity he knew how to satisfy.

Brandy was different. She didn't inflame his libido. Well, maybe she did. A little. Still, when he looked at her, his thoughts didn't veer directly into the bedroom. Her rigid posture made him wonder why she was so tense. The uncertainty in her eyes made him long to throttle the person who had put it there. Dammit, he wanted to know what her problem was.

And he wanted to fix it.

He was rattled by the loaded silence that stretched out in the freeze-frame moment. Unnerved by a fierce protectiveness he didn't want to feel. Trick cleared the tightness from his throat. "Can I help you, Ms. Mitchum?"

Her gaze flitted around the cluttered office. "I believe you're the one who could use help, Mr. Templeton."

"Why's that?"

She smiled. "Well, unless a cyclone I didn't hear about blew through town recently, you need a good organizer."

"Who do you have in mind?"

"Me."

"The other night you couldn't even talk to me. Wouldn't helping me violate your professional ethics?"

She shrugged dismissively. "Not anymore. I no longer work for Futterman-Ulbright."

That got his attention. "You quit?"

"No." She hesitated. Swallowed. "I was fired."

"What happened?"

"Futterman went ballistic because a document I prepared for a pretrial conference looked more like a cryptogram than a list of contentions."

"I can see where that might be a problem." He leaned back in his chair. "It's never a good idea to bungle your boss's briefs."

She blinked, and her lower lip trembled. He'd made a stupid joke, but she'd assumed it was an insinuation. "It wasn't a brief. And what's more, I didn't bungle anything. I don't know what went wrong. Something. The bottom line is, through no real fault of my own, I find myself unemployed."

And none too happy about that state of affairs. Affairs? Now there was a word he had to keep out of his mind and vocabulary where this woman was concerned. "Have a seat, Ms. Mitchum."

She looked around and grimaced. "Where?"

"I think there's a chair somewhere under these binders." He stepped around the desk, reaching for a teetering stack of report folders. She tried to move them at the same time, and their hands touched. A nothing brush of skin against skin, but it cranked up his heart rate, and accelerated his pulse into a dangerous high-pressure zone.

"I don't understand. This isn't a law firm," he pointed out unnecessarily as he returned to his seat. He hated to prove Ace right by being difficult, but the recent string of strange, just-outside-the-realm-of-coincidence events had left him off balance. *She* left him off balance. Unfamiliar emotions and unseemly attraction was a volatile combination. He knew how to control a raging oil well fire, but didn't know the first thing about getting a handle on traitorous, neck-up, *romantic* feelings that could burn him just as badly.

"I know." Brandy sat on the edge of the seat he'd cleared, tentative and uneasy. Her back was stiff as rebar as she clutched the purse in her lap.

"Don't you want to be a paralegal anymore?"

His question kindled a small, smoky flame in her eyes, but she quickly extinguished it. "Yes, I do. But there aren't any available paralegal positions in Odessa right now."

"So you're willing to . . . what? Settle for less?"

She was silent for a moment. "Being a paralegal is a dream. Dreams don't pay the bills. Jobs do. I have other skills." Her chin edged up. "I fit your requirements."

She's exactly what you need. Again, the thought came out of nowhere. Like a tickle of warm breath on the back of his neck, it increased Trick's discomfort. He slapped his neck, expecting to see a squashed mosquito on his clean palm. "And how do you know what I require?"

She plopped her purse on the desk, opened the clasp and removed a folded piece of paper, which she handed to him. He looked it over, surprised to see his company's name on the job opening printout. "I don't know how you got this. I never contacted Flash, or any other personnel agency."

"Maybe someone else in your firm did," she suggested hopefully.

Ace. He'd been nagging Trick for days to face the fact that Wylodene was gone for good. The old man wasn't the sneaky type. He usually slapped his cards on the table.

But he *was* stubborn and set in his ways and just plain ornery enough to take it upon himself to intervene.

"Maybe," Trick allowed. "Tell me, Ms. Mitchum, do you want to work for me?"

She took a deep breath. "Can we be honest here?"

"I think we should, don't you?"

She nodded. Gulped. "Okay. I don't really want to work for you. Honestly, you make me nervous. Every time I'm around you, I get the feeling that . . . well, that there's a bomb ticking in the background."

"A bomb?"

"Not a literal bomb." She nailed him with that earnest, you-can-trust-me smile. "However, I have a child to feed and debts to pay. I need a job. You need an office manager."

"So if I scratch your back, you'll scratch mine?"

She took a quick breath. "If I take the job, I prefer no body parts be involved. Are we clear on that?" When he nodded, she continued. "I've had enough melodrama in my life lately, can we cut to the chase?"

"Cut away."

"Do you want me or not?"

He wanted her. More than he cared to admit. Unflinching, she held the intimidating stare he'd perfected on men twice her size and ten times as tough. As one fighter to another, he had to admire Brandy's spirit. If she could stand her ground and face him down, she could handle the crew's rough ways and keep up with the chaotic pace of the business.

The silence dragged out too long. "You're my best chance," she finally admitted, her voice edged with resignation.

He did not want to hear that. He couldn't be anyone's best chance. Ever. "You don't play poker, do you, Ms. Mitchum?"

"No, I don't."

"I didn't think so. If you did, you'd know better than to show your hand so early in the game."

She leaned forward, her palms braced on his desktop, her dark eyes staring into his soul. "Let's get something straight, Mr. Templeton. This is not a game. It's my life. My child's life." She took another paper out of her purse and dropped it on his desk. "Here's my résumé. As you can see, I have plenty of experience. I've worked since I was fourteen, and I work hard. I'm reliable, and I take my job seriously."

He skimmed the document. "You've also been fired a few times." He was impressed by the unflinching honesty that allowed her to include dismissals on her résumé.

A hot itch formed between his shoulder blades, as if unseen eyes were boring into his back. *You'll always know where you stand with her.* He half turned in his chair and looked. Of course, nobody was there. He casually rubbed his back against the chair. Something was sure as hell making him twitchy. Maybe he shouldn't have had that second cup of Ace's death-by-caffeine coffee.

"That's right," she said quietly. "I've been fired. Because I've made caring for Chloe a priority."

"I don't get it."

"Why should you? You're male. Fathering a child doesn't limit a man's options. Mothering a child almost always limits a woman's. If we choose career fulfillment, we're labeled bad mothers. If we do right by our children, we're condemned for not being ambitious enough. I'm a good mother. I love my daughter. That does not mean I can't do this job."

The words sounded practiced, but sincere. She'd defended motherhood before. Probably more than once. So she'd already learned the life-isn't-fair lesson. Trick had found that doing the right thing was no guarantee of reward. Sometimes the "reward" was pain. Loss. He sensed fear would not stop this young woman from doing the right thing. Especially when it came to her child.

How different his life might have been had his own mother possessed half Brandy's dedication. If Liz Templeton had made her only child a priority, he might not have lost her so soon. Had she stayed home to care for him instead of rushing to Colombia to join Buck at a well-fire site, she would not have been on the company plane when it went down in the jungle. Trick had been ten years old at the time.

Young enough to need her. To miss her. Old enough to harden his heart against loss.

Eleven years later, Buck was killed in a well explosion in the Middle East, leaving Trick on his own. He'd run Hotspur and his life ever since, alone and without help. Just the way he liked it.

Because you're too hardheaded to know better.

The itch returned. He refused to turn around again and confront an empty office. He rolled his shoulders. *What's so great about being alone?* That was it. He was definitely cutting back on caffeine. Maybe a nice cup of herbal tea in the mornings —

"So? How about it?" she pressed. "Are you willing to give me a chance?"

Did he dare? She could do the job. No question. Based on her résumé and what he knew about her personality, she would be an asset to the company. Like everything he did, his hesitation was self-motivated. The plain truth was, he was reluctant to offer the chance she wanted for fear he couldn't resist the temptation of her. Was he strong enough? Good enough? Could he see her every day and treat her with the professional respect she deserved? He'd have to say no to the unlikely stirrings he felt for her. Do the right thing, no matter what the "reward." He wasn't sure he possessed that much integrity.

In the past, it had been easy to remain honorable in his dealings with women. They didn't get hurt because he let them know exactly what to expect from him.

A good time tonight and no tomorrows.

"Do I have to beg, Templeton?"

Brandy's plaintive question sucked him back into the moment. "No, Ms. Mitchum. You don't. I do need someone to run the office." Briefly he told her about Wylodene and how things at Hotspur had unraveled since the older woman had acted on rash romantic impulses.

"Your office manager gave you no notice of her intentions?"

Brandy's gentle tone let him know she would never hang him out to dry. He *would* always know where he stood with her. Damn! Was this how it started? Was he already depending on her? "Yeah, I guess she did give me notice. I didn't believe she'd really leave."

"I understand why you're reluctant to hire me," she said.

"I doubt that." How could she? He didn't fully understand his reasons himself. He pushed to his feet and paced, caught between wanting to help her and fearing he'd hurt her. If there was one thing Brandy Mitchum didn't deserve, it was an additional serving of hurt. He caught the scent of cinnamon again when he passed her chair. Maybe the scent was coming from her. Damn, the woman was so sweet she smelled like cookies. He was in big trouble.

"But I do," she insisted. "You've already lost one employee due to a personal conflict. I don't blame you for being nervous about hiring someone with so many responsibilities."

"That's not —"

"Let me assure you. I've been on my

own a long time. My mother was sick a lot when I was growing up. I learned to be independent, even when I was married to Chloe's father. He didn't help out much. The day Chloe was born, I worked all day, drove myself to the hospital and went through labor without him. Trust me. I can manage on my own."

She seemed to hold her breath, awaiting his decision. Damn, after that heartbreak of a life story, what else could he do? He propped one hip on the desk and spoke with all the enthusiasm he could muster. Which wasn't much. "Is a salary of forty thousand dollars a year acceptable?"

"Oh, yes." Relief transformed her face from wary to radiant. "With medical insurance benefits and regular reviews for raises?"

What was he doing? "Okay. Sure. The job's yours. With a few conditions."

"Right." Her smile crumbled, as she braced herself for bad news. "There are always conditions."

"First of all," he said with a calculated gruffness he didn't feel, "I want you out of this office no later than 5:30 p.m. every day."

"What?"

The gratitude in her eyes squeezed his

heart like a fist. He blustered past the unnerving feeling that he'd become her Santa Claus today. "You heard me. Company policy. No overtime. No weekends, either. That clear?"

"Yes, sir. Whatever you say."

"My other condition is that you continue looking for a paralegal position. If you find one, take it. Just give me a week's notice and train your replacement."

Her doe's eyes were guarded again. "Do you mean this is only a temporary position?" Why did she have to look like she'd expected him to pull the rug out from under her?

"It's as permanent as you want it to be," he explained. "All I meant was, if you find a job you'd rather do, something more fulfilling, I want you to feel free to pursue it. No strings attached. No hard feelings."

She stood, and though he didn't see her brush her purse, it fell to the floor. They reached for it at the same time. Their hands brushed again, then clasped like magnets on metal. Their eyes met, and he could tell she was as affected by the contact as he was.

She snatched her hand away. "Thank you, Mr. Templeton. So much." He passed her the bag, and she set the strap over her shoulder. For a second, he thought she might extend her hand for the obligatory handshake, but she hesitated, reconsidered. "You are saving my life."

Relief flickered through him. He didn't have to touch her again. Good. Touching her opened a floodgate of insistent, whispering memories. Which was absurd. They hadn't known each other long enough or well enough to share memories. "I don't think it's clear who's rescuing whom here."

She smiled as relief dissolved worry. Making someone else happy felt good. Maybe he should try it more often. "Thank you again," she said. "You won't regret this."

That's what she thought. He already regretted letting her into his life, even if it was just into his office. Why, he didn't know. He'd given her the same terms he always gave women. Stay as long as it's comfortable. Until something better comes along. Then split. No hurt feelings, no recriminations. Don't look back. The only difference was, this time the conditions were occupational, not personal. Which added a new wrinkle to things.

There was only one way this arrangement would work. They could only have one kind of relationship — employee-employer.

He'd have to do the right thing from here on out. Be on his best behavior. No thinking unseemly thoughts. No giving in to the longing that warmed his blood when this intriguing, unsuitable-for-him woman was around.

Damn! He'd just made a flash-fire decision that would complicate his life in ways he couldn't begin to imagine. Pretty stupid for a guy who liked to keep things simple. Then again, maybe the decision to hire Brandy Mitchum had not been totally his.

Ridiculous. He was his own man. The boss. Had been for years. There were no outside forces urging him along, prompting him to act. Still, impulsivity came with a price.

The situation had disaster stamped all over it.

What the hell had he gotten himself into?

"Call me Trick. We don't stand on formality around here. When can you start?"

"Right now?" Brandy smiled again, and her undisguised joy grabbed his heart. Wouldn't let go. She'd make a lousy poker player. Easy to read. Easy to take advantage of.

Easy to hurt, too, and don't forget it.

"Good enough." He strode to the door,

knowing Ace probably had one ear pressed against it. He yanked it open, and the old man nearly tumbled to the floor.

"Give a feller some warning, boss," Ace grumbled. "I can't afford to break any bones at my age."

"That's what you get for eavesdropping." He introduced Hotspur's oldest employee to its newest. "Ms. Mitchum is our new office manager. Show her the ropes and get her started."

"You got it." Ace turned from Brandy and flashed Trick an approving wink. "You done the right thing, boss."

So what if he had? No need getting giddy about it. Whether this "right thing" proved reward or punishment remained to be seen. Trick didn't know whether to be grateful to the old man for posting the help wanted ad or mad at him for taking the matter into his own hands.

"I have a bone to pick with you, Ace, but it'll have to wait. I gotta get out to the field."

"You go right ahead, boss. We'll be fine, won't we, Ms. Mitchum?"

"Brandy. I understand you don't stand on formalities around here."

"That's an understatement." Ace cackled.

The gratitude shimmering in Brandy's

eyes melted what little resolve Trick had left. "Thank you again, Trick. For taking a chance on me."

That was the understatement. He was definitely taking a chance. A big one. He'd been called fearless, but he wasn't reckless. Or careless. He always calculated the odds carefully before acting. He didn't step into harm's way without being absolutely certain of the outcome. Failure was never an option.

Until now. Letting Brandy Mitchum, with her precocious child and her prickly problems and her spunky independence into his life was the biggest gamble he'd ever taken. He wasn't ready. He was used to risking his neck, not his emotions. Someone could get hurt here. And that someone could be him.

The drapes fluttered again. *You're a big boy. You can handle yourself.* Overwhelming awareness suddenly tensed every muscle. Trick was standing too close to Brandy. The elusive cinnamon scent was enveloped by the fresh, fruity smell of her shampoo. Her shiny hair reflected the light like polished mahogany. Her full, lush lips . . . he was definitely too close. He'd better have someone come in and check that draft. Might not hurt to have his head examined too.

127

He stepped back, cleared his throat again. "You have no idea what you're getting into." He spoke to Brandy, but addressed the comment to himself. As if he ever took his own advice.

"Oh, I think I do." Her bright, happy smile created a spark. Not in his loins where it could be safely confined, but in his heart. It was a fire he wasn't sure he could fight, smoldering in a place where he'd never allowed a flame to grow.

Brandy followed Ace down the hall. She couldn't believe her good luck but wasn't about to question the turn of events. An hour ago, she'd considered giving up on Odessa and moving home. Something had conspired to change bottom-of-the-barrel resignation to top-of-the-world optimism. Fate or coincidence? Luck or miracle? Life was an adventure, full of surprises. Some scary, some pleasant. Some downright puzzling.

Trick Templeton was all those things. He'd been a stranger, albeit an eerily familiar one, when she'd first encountered him on the road four days ago. She'd run into him time after time. She may even have seen him in her dreams. Now he was her employer. She'd never considered herself a damsel in distress, but if the scenario had played out in the pages of one of Chloe's storybooks, Trick would definitely be a knight in shining armor. A reluctant one, who wasn't all that enthusiastic about the role.

It was comforting to believe in fairy tales. Easy to think their fates were somehow entwined. That the domino fall of recent events had happened for a reason. Either she was meant to be here, or stress had made her nuts. Nagged by fatalistic thoughts, she accompanied the old man to her new workstation. She immediately felt at home in Hotspur's front office. The cream-colored walls soaked up the morning light pouring through open wooden blinds. The desk was large, and black filing cabinets lined one wall. On the wall opposite, framed photos documented Hotspur history. An organized mind had arranged the space. She could do good work here.

"That there's the supply closet," Ace pointed out. "There's a private ladies' room next to it."

The phone rang, and Ace took the phone call. Brandy excused herself and ducked into the restroom. The confidence she'd tried to maintain in front of Trick was rapidly evaporating. She needed to pull herself together.

Like a cat that hadn't quite used up all its lives, she'd landed on her feet again. Still, the near disaster had left her shaken. She leaned against the closed door, her legs weak and her heart pounding. This must be how death-row inmates felt when the governor granted a reprieve at the last moment. She looked at her watch. It wasn't even 11:00 a.m. Not counting the weekend, she'd been unemployed less than three hours before landing another position. A good position. With a decent salary and insurance benefits. Close to home.

As Mr. Johnson, the employment counselor had said, the job seemed made in heaven. Best of all, she'd be working for a man who didn't expect her to live at the office, one whose company policy forbade overtime. Amazing. But then, a lot of amazing things had happened the past few days.

All she had to do was ignore the impossible attraction she felt for her new boss. That should be easy. He scared the molasses out of her. Yet she was drawn to him. Moth to flame. Great. She was turning into a cliché.

She'd been so worried about losing her

job that she hadn't spent much time considering the weird little cosmic nudges that had led her back to Trick Templeton. Nor did she have time to think about them now. She tucked a stray wisp of hair into her braid, reapplied her lipstick and powdered her nose before rejoining Ace.

She'd regained the appearance of normalcy, but the wily old man zeroed right in on the source of her discomfort.

"He ain't so bad."

"Who?"

"Trick. His bark is way worse than his bite. Nothing to be scared of."

"I'll try to remember that." The old man showed her how to work the phones before he excused himself. After he left, Brandy checked out the contents of the files, looked in the desk drawers. Tried to feel at home in her new job.

Nothing to be afraid of. Ace's words echoed in her mind, but he was dead wrong. Trick was everything that had ever scared her away from a man. Too handsome. Too bossy. Too intense. Tough and accustomed to getting his way. She knew what she wanted, and he wasn't it.

Thank goodness, he was her boss. Even if he weren't, she was smart enough not to get involved with him. After a disastrous

131

marriage to a man who could not accept responsibility, she was ready for a quiet life. No excitement required. The last thing she needed was a worldly, no-strings-attached nomad. Templeton was the polar opposite of the minivan-driving, stable nice guy she pictured in her future.

Trick embraced danger on a daily basis. She wanted a man who walked on the dull side. An insurance adjuster would be nice. Or an accountant. A gentle man, more familiar with debits and credits than hellfire infernos. One who valued marriage and would help rear Chloe. Maybe a couple more kids down the line.

What she didn't want — and certainly didn't need — was some hotshot adventure junkie on the prowl for his next adrenaline fix.

Even if touching him put her in the center of a magic spell.

Everyone knew magic wasn't real. Neither were dreams, or the men who populated them. She couldn't afford to risk her future, and Chloe's, on a sexy illusion.

Chapter Six

The next morning, Brandy accompanied Chloe to her classroom as usual. Her nocturnal visitor had failed to put in an appearance last night. He must have had a prior engagement to heat up some other lonely woman's dreams. She should have been relieved. After all, she'd slept soundly for the first time in over a week. Instead, she'd awakened feeling abandoned and bereft.

She squeezed Chloe's hand gently, comforted by her daughter's warmth. This was the real world. Work was real. Paying bills was real. The Midnight Man was nothing more than a grownup version of an imaginary playmate. A figment of her secret longings.

When they reached the primary wing, a small boy galloped past, then turned around and grinned. Walking backward down the hallway, he called out in a teasing, singsong manner. "Good morning, Chloe."

"Hello, Spencer." Chloe's tight tone meant she knew what was coming.

"Did you bring the Invisible Man to school today, weirdo?" The jeering taunt was accompanied by mocking, woo woo sound effects. Laughing, Spencer pivoted on his heel and raced down the corridor, red lights flashing on his expensive sneakers.

"Boys," Chloe muttered. "They're so dumb!"

Brandy patted Chloe's shoulder. "He was just teasing." Her stomach had cramped all morning at the prospect of working for Trick Templeton. Now her heart ached too. Spencer's taunt about Celestian had been Chloe's Introduction to Harsh Reality 101. She would face bigger disappointments in life. Worse hurts. Maybe retreating into an imaginary world was a good idea.

No. Chloe was strong. She would cope. "Don't let Spencer hurt your feelings."

"He can't, unless I let him."

Brandy smiled. "That's my girl. Not just smart but wise to boot. Do you think maybe Celestian could stay home?" The imaginary friend had caused Chloe nothing but trouble, but considering how much Brandy missed the tall, dark comfort of her dreams, she could hardly ask her daughter to give him up completely.

Chloe paused at the door of her classroom and yanked on her mother's sleeve. She lowered her voice so the parents and children passing in and out couldn't hear. "You're right, Mommy. I don't really need Celestian's help at school."

Hoping this was the beginning of the end for the imaginary friend, Brandy knelt on one knee, grasped her daughter's shoulders and looked her in the eye. "I *never* thought you needed help. You're such a clever girl. You'll do just fine on your own."

Chloe nodded. "I can handle kindergarten and Miss Steuban. Celestian should go with you today and help you at your new work."

"That's very generous of you." Brandy's heart swelled with love.

"I know." She leaned close and whispered behind her hand. "He can be a big pain in the you-know-what, but he knows stuff."

"That's good," Brandy whispered back with a smile. "Because I have no idea what I'll have to do today."

Trick Templeton had given her a chance, but what if she blew it? If she proved incompetent, would he kick her to the curb? The threat of super-sizing fry orders for a

135

living loomed over her like a black cloud.

"Are you ever scared, Mommy?" Chloe asked softly.

"Of course I am, baby. All the time."

Chloe's eyes widened. "But you always act brave!"

"Being brave doesn't mean you're not afraid. Being brave means standing up to what frightens you." It meant working for an intimidating man because you needed the job, even if he gave you all kinds of goose bumps.

"Oh. I get it now. Celestian!" Chloe's whispered summons was as full of authority as a five-year-old could make it. "Go with Mommy." Her grin was smug. "I'm his boss. He has to do what I say. Don't worry. He'll be there."

"I'm glad." Brandy relaxed a little. Maybe this was Chloe's way of letting go of the fantasy. Of moving on. Now maybe she wouldn't have to suffer Spencer's bratty scorn today.

"Remember, Mommy, if you have a problem, just let Celestian help you."

Today was too important to trust to imaginary friends, so Brandy sent up a silent prayer. Don't let me blow this chance! The sweet, familiar smell of cinnamon made her think she had an answer. Then she noticed a little girl munching on teddy bear crackers as she walked by and chided herself. Reality. Focus.

"Is that okay, Mommy?"

Brandy gave Chloe a hug. If her daughter wanted to let go of Celestian, she would play along. "Sure, baby, I can use all the help I can get."

Chloe sighed wearily and unshouldered her Barbie backpack. "Good, 'cause I can really use a break."

Brandy began to think her prayers had been answered after all. During her first week on the job, Trick Templeton's demanding schedule kept him in the field and out of her path. Without his sexy, brooding presence around to distract her, she quickly restored order to the front office. Chloe insisted Celestian had arranged for Brandy's position at Hotspur and was stubbornly adamant that he had to help her do a good job. Therefore, every day was Take Your Daughter's Imaginary Friend to Work Day.

Sometimes she was amazed at how well she adapted to a new routine, but she had Ace to help, not Chloe's Celestian. It was the grizzled firefighter who taught her the basics of the well control operation.

"So what do you think?" It was Friday morning, and he'd just carried in the mail from Hotspur's post office box.

Brandy looked up from the computer screen and smiled. She liked Ace. He was full of stories and bluster, but had a soft heart. "About what?"

"Hotspur. Reckon you'll stay?"

"I reckon." She sorted the envelopes he'd placed on her desk.

"Good. You 'bout got Wylodene's system figured out?"

"I think so." Her predecessor had set up a computerized bookkeeping program to manage payroll and track daily income and expense transactions. All Brandy had to do was forward weekly summary reports to a local accounting firm where a CPA balanced the books and filed the required tax reports. Even though she hadn't used the software before, it had seemed oddly familiar. Like something she'd once mastered and hadn't quite forgotten. "It's amazing in its simplicity."

Ace nodded. "I knew you was smart, first time I saw you. I said to myself, that gal's got a lot on the ball."

"Why, thank you, Ace."

"If you have the payroll ready, I've got time to run it out to the boys at the barn."

"Right here." Brandy handed him a large envelope containing the crew's paychecks. Between jobs, the men worked out of a "war room" in the equipment barn outside town. Most had already found an excuse to stop by and welcome her aboard. Like Ace, they were a friendly lot, a little rough around the edges, but kind and well meaning.

When the old fellow tucked the envelope under his arm but made no move to leave, Brandy asked, "Did I forget something?"

"Nope. You're doing a slam-bang job."

"That's means a lot, coming from someone whose opinion I value."

His seamed face flushed. "Trick oughta have told you so himself."

"He's been busy this week."

"No excuse. So I'm telling you. You're a good'un." He ducked his head in embarrassment. "Yep, well, I'll head on out then." He slapped his beat-up cowboy hat on his head. At the door, he turned back and winked. "We're all glad you're here. Even us'n who don't say so."

It was nice to feel appreciated for a change. Brandy smiled as Ace drove off. He was a sweet old guy. A lifelong bachelor with no family, who claimed Hotspur was his home. He'd been grateful for the cookies she'd brought in yesterday. His only complaint was that Trick hadn't been around to share them. Templeton had to be a good man, if good men thought so highly of him.

Trick stopped by the office several times that first week to sign contracts or grab messages and return calls. He hardly slowed down as he whizzed past Brandy's desk. He didn't wait for an answer to his question about how things were going, he just muttered "good job" before rushing on. He was always alert for the next fire to put out. Literally and figuratively.

Like a dust devil on the plains, Trick was in constant motion, stirring up everything around him. Leaving Brandy breathless in his wake. Jumpy physical awareness made her heart gallop whenever he was under the same roof. Fortunately for her peace of mind, he was away from the office more than he was around. He didn't believe in downtime and kept his highly paid crews busy by accepting every job that came along, no matter how dangerous. He seemed to get a steady adrenaline fix fighting infernos that would terrify the average man. If she'd learned one thing about the uncommunicative and intensely private man she worked for, it was that he was far from average.

No doubt, Ace had reported favorably on her performance, because Trick seemed content to let her manage the office without much supervision. She reveled in the autonomy. Unlike her previous boss, Trick was competent and trusted others to be competent too. Every one of his men made a point of telling her what a fine boss he was. Unlike Fenton Futterman. By all accounts, Trick was intelligent and street-smart. Tough as nails when he had to be, fair and reasonable the rest of the time. From what she'd heard, he didn't have to build himself up by tearing others down.

According to Ace, Trick knew the business inside and out, and had an instinct for fires that was, as the old hellfighter put it, as rare as frog hair.

The Hotspur crew answered an emergency call-out to a fire site in New Mexico the next week. Ace manned the equipment barn, leaving Brandy on her own. She missed the legal profession but enjoyed working at Hotspur. Understanding tasks came easily. Maybe a little too easily. She knew exactly where to locate needed documents. She picked up industry jargon from the reports she typed and conversed knowledgeably with clients. Not so weird. She was, after all, a fast learner.

Brandy had played along with Chloe about letting Celestian help her at the office, but at times it *did* seem like someone with a stake in her success was working beside her, whispering in her ear, silently feeding her information. Even when she was the only one in the office, she never felt alone. Instead of creeping her out, the sensation was comforting. Like the presence of the dark man in her dreams had been. The Midnight Man must have jumped ship completely, because he'd been AWOL since she started at Hotspur.

Practical and focused on success, Brandy dismissed uneasy feelings about her office "assistant," just as she'd dismissed déjà vu moments with Trick. She was happy. She no longer worked after hours. No one pressured her to come in early, to work through lunch or to stay late. She left Hotspur promptly at five, relaxed and eager to spend time with her daughter instead of anxious and uncertain. As enjoyable as the sudden peace was, it left her with an uneasy prickling sensation. In her experience, life never ran too smoothly for long.

Celestian was still an important part of Chloe's life. He no longer accompanied her to school, but she carried on lengthy one-sided monologues and consulted him on childish matters of state over tea parties in her room.

One night, Brandy stood outside the door after she'd tucked her daughter in and shamelessly eavesdropped.

"I don't like it when Mommy has problems," Chloe whispered.

Brandy pressed her ear against the door. After a few seconds, she heard Chloe speak again. "What do you mean domestic distress? I don't understand that."

Silence.

"Oh, I get it. Trick can help. I guess that's okay."

Brandy leaned heavily against the wall. Why was Chloe talking to herself? She was probably talking to her invisible friend, but that was worse. Poor kid. Worrying about domestic problems? Maybe she shouldn't have mentioned the trouble she'd been having with the dryer. Chloe was sensitive and picked up on things that wouldn't even appear on most kids' radars.

Brandy set the alarm clock and climbed into bed. Things had been going a little too well. The cosmos demanded balance, and so her clothes dryer had started acting up. Its achy thumps and groans were too ominous for normal wear and tear, but she didn't want to spend money on it until she had to. She'd opened a savings account with the severance pay from Futterman and hoped she wouldn't have to spend the funds for a new dryer.

Maybe it was a mistake to play along about Celestian, but the idea of an omnipotent imaginary friend could very well be Chloe's way of exerting control over her life. Primitive people created imaginative explanations for things they didn't understand. Maybe Celestian was Chloe's way of making sense of her life. She couldn't take that away from her.

But she could get her daughter involved in more activities. If she enrolled Chloe in a Saturday morning dance class, the issue might resolve itself once she developed other interests and made new friends.

Good plan. Brandy punched up her pillow. Now all she had to do was come up with a way to make herself stop thinking about Trick Templeton.

Late Friday afternoon, Brandy was finishing up for the day and worrying about the stupid dryer. It had finally given up the ghost. She could pay for repairs by taking money out of savings, but if it was truly *el morte*, she didn't know what to do. She was considering her options when Trick burst through the front door.

"You're back!" Oh, boy! Oh, no!

"Just got in." Without slowing for chit-chat, he strode past her desk. "I need to make some calls. Give me a few minutes, then come and fill me in on what happened while I was gone."

His unexpected appearance totally unnerved her. The crew wasn't due back in town for a couple of days. It must have taken less time than estimated to cap the titan blowout. Not surprising, considering how good Trick was at his job, but still, a little advance warning of an imminent barge-in would have been nice. Except she didn't own the place. *He* did. Best remember that.

She printed the invoice she'd just finished and stamped the outgoing mail. After clearing her desk for the weekend, she turned off the computer and picked up an EPA report for Trick's signature.

She swigged a gulp of cinnamon-flavored tea to steady her nerves. Since she began working here, she couldn't get enough of the stuff. The warm, spicy scent seemed to linger in the air, even when she hadn't brewed a cup for a while. She used the same brand she'd always used, but the tea

had never had such a lingering effect before. Had to be the way the office air ducts
were configured or something.

She gathered Trick's messages and
walked down the hall to his office. He was
on the phone. She paused outside the
door, but he waved her to a chair while he
finished discussing the impending lawsuit
with his attorney.

"Well, Charles, sometimes no news *isn't*
good news," he muttered. "Yeah, I know.
The wheels of justice turn slowly. You
know me, slow is not how I like to do
things. The legal system would lose in a
footrace with a glacier. Just call me when
you hear something."

He dropped the receiver into the cradle
and looked up. His bronzed skin reflected
his recent days in the sun. The tiny lines
around his mouth and eyes were etched a
little deeper. Sometimes she forgot that he
was nine years older than her. More
worldly. Far more experienced. "So how're
you doing?"

He needed a trim, but scissors would
ruin his dark hair's touchable lack of style.
The untamed look suited him. He didn't
think much about his appearance, but
anyone who looked that good didn't have
to. His question was perfectly respectable,

and yet his hard body spoke to hers. She quivered under an onslaught of sensations. She swallowed hard before speaking. Never let 'em see you drool. "I'm fine."

"Glad somebody is."

"Charles is right about the wheels of justice," she pointed out. "The only time they move quickly is when you *don't* want them to."

"So I'm learning. So, what's it been now? A couple of weeks since you started?"

"More or less."

"Can't you find a paralegal job?"

She stiffened. "I'm not looking for a paralegal job." Did he expect her to quit? If so, he didn't know her very well. Why trade a bird in the hand for two in the unemployment line? The devil you knew was less intimidating than the one you didn't.

"All that training? Money spent for classes? Are you just planning to give that up?" He actually seemed interested. She didn't think he ever considered her in any context except how she could make his business run more smoothly.

"No. I plan to keep my hand in by volunteering a few hours a week at legal aid."

"You have time for that?"

Her old defensiveness fluttered. "I promise nothing I do on my own time will interfere with my duties here. Chloe spends every other weekend with her father. I'll volunteer while she's gone."

"Right. So you're not planning to leave me, er, Hotspur anytime soon?"

In the instant before his indifferent poker face took over, she glimpsed something wistful in his expression. Was that vulnerability she'd seen buried under layers of arrogant attitude and brash bearing? If so, he was far better at bluffing than she, but she suddenly knew he was hiding something. The thought smashed through her defenses and brought her hackles to heel.

Trick Templeton wasn't invincible. He had feelings. He could be hurt. Most amazing of all, was the uncanny realization that she could be the one who hurt him. In what universe could that ever happen? "Not unless you want me to," she said softly. He nodded. That must have been the right answer.

"Just so you know, I think you're doing a good job running the front office." His brows drew down in one of his trademark scowls. He cleared his throat to loosen the compliment that had stuck in his craw. "So far."

"Thank you." She glanced at the phone.

"I take it from your conversation that you don't have a court date yet?"

"No. Charles says it could be a while."

"Futterman's probably stalling. He hates going to court. He's an expert at using the water-on-rock approach."

"What?"

"Trying to wear you down with waiting so you'll settle."

"When hell freezes over."

"Have you considered mediation?"

He scoffed. "Never gonna happen."

"You know, in a case like this, compromise might be the answer."

"I don't compromise. I fight. And win."

She definitely felt like the loser where he was concerned. She'd seen a chink in his armor, but hadn't had the courage to chip it away. "When do you give your deposition?"

"I don't know. Charles says be patient." He groaned and stretched his arms behind his head as though relieving a cramp or stiff muscle. Dressed in worn blue jeans, faded denim shirt and scuffed boots, he looked more like a ranch hand than a successful businessman. A well-developed, muscular, appealing ranch hand.

Brandy shuffled the stack of pink While You Were Out message slips. Her heart thumped in her chest. A little additional oxygen wouldn't go amiss. The more time she spent with Trick, the harder it was to breathe. "Patience isn't one of your strong points, is it?"

"What do you mean?" He rocked forward, and reached for the messages.

"From what I've seen, you only have two speeds."

"And in your opinion, those are . . ." He flipped through the slips, tossed them on his desk and looked up expectantly.

"Raring to go and champing at the bit."

Rich laughter startled and warmed her. His dark gaze held hers. "You're wrong about that. I can go slowly when the need arises. Some things shouldn't be rushed."

"Right." The image of Trick's "rising needs" and him engaged in one of those slow, leisurely activities sent a red hot flush to her face and a shiver down her spine. Great. Now she was stuck with the love-making visual.

He smiled. Was he aware of her discomfort? Probably not. He was a pro at maintaining proper employer-employee protocol. She was imagining things again. "Take a good meal for example," he said. "I like to linger. Relish the flavors. Savor every bite. Experience every tasty morsel.

Of course, I haven't had a good, home-cooked dinner for a long time."

"Ah . . . that's too bad." His smile was rueful. She ached to serve him something that would satisfy the hunger in his eyes. She could invite him over. For dinner. She was a pretty good cook, but didn't have much opportunity to show off her skills. Chloe's tastes were tame. As a matter of fact, so were hers. Inviting Trick for anything, even dinner, was not a good idea. She broke eye contact and stared at her hands as the flush spread and washed her entire body in heat. Good grief. She wasn't exactly thinking about food.

"Do you have something for me?" he asked.

"No!" She looked up. His assessing gaze made her breath jam in her lungs. "I'm not really your type."

He gestured in her direction. "Is that for me?"

"Wh-what?" She was stammering. And her mouth was running. Cripes! She was losing it. Normally she was so sensible where men were concerned. Ten minutes with Trick and she was blabbering like a seventh-grader talking to a "cute boy" on the bus. Maybe he hadn't noticed. He probably got that reaction from women all the time.

"Is there a problem?" he asked.

"Well, yeah. I think we're too different is all. We don't really have that much in common." She regretted her words as soon as they blurted out. It had to be oxygen deprivation. She snatched a quick breath. "Uh, I didn't —"

Amusement danced in his eyes, but he soberly pointed to the folder tucked under her arm. "I meant that." At least he didn't laugh in her face.

Obviously, her overactive imagination made her read something into his question that simply was not there. If there were any magic in the world, right about now would be a good time for her fairy godmother to swirl her off to another dimension. Anything to get her out of here. "Right. EPA report." She laid it on his desk blotter and stood. "After you read it, sign on the last page and leave it on my desk."

"Anything else I need to know?"

"Um. No." Egad. Hadn't she said enough already? "Nothing important."

"Anything unimportant?"

His lazy appraisal swept from the French braid on her head to the leather pumps on her feet, heating her blood and nearly making her sway. If she wanted to continue working for this man, she had to stop having complete physical meltdowns in his presence. She had to stop imagining him in her bedroom.

Sitting on the edge of her bed. Touching her. That's what dream men were for.

"This isn't a law firm," he reminded her.

"I know."

"So you don't have to wear suits and pointy-toed shoes to work. In case you haven't noticed, the dress code is a little more relaxed around here."

There went that imagination again. He'd been checking out her attire, not her, she realized a bit sadly. No. Gladly. "Relaxed?" The word didn't begin to describe the current situation. She was standing, but movement was probably too much to expect with so many randomly firing neurons.

"Wylodene maintained decorum in jeans and Western shirts she sewed herself. You can take your wardrobe down a notch, if you want."

Yeah, well, so could he. Fifteen notches lower on the sex appeal meter would be appreciated. Then she might stop making a fool of herself. "Thank you. I'll keep that in mind." Silence swelled between them. Throbbed like a beating heart. Okay, maybe fifty notches. She wanted to leave but couldn't get the message from her short-circuited brain to her paralyzed feet.

The only body part that seemed to be in complete working order was her big mouth. And her nose. Was her imagination running amok again, or was the cinnamon scent even stronger than it had been earlier? Before she could clamp down on it, another dumb question popped out. "Do you know a reliable appliance repairman in town?"

"I might. What's malfunctioning?"

My brain. My heart. Oh, and my stomach. She was so nervous, there was a chance she might actually throw up if she didn't get away from him soon. Not a good way to impress a man. Except he wasn't just any man; he was her boss. Whole different critter, and she'd better not forget it. "Clothes dryer. It's been making a funny noise for a week or so, and this afternoon when I went home on my lunch hour, it wouldn't work at all."

"Is it out of warranty?"

"Uh, yeah. For five years."

"Did you check the circuit breaker?" he asked.

"Yes, I did. Circuits are all accounted for."

"Does the drum turn?"

"What?"

"The part that goes around." He made the appropriate gesture with a long index finger. "Does it turn?"

"No. When I push the power button, nothing happens."

"Sounds like a broken belt." He glanced at his battered wristwatch. "It's nearly five. You probably won't get anyone out until next week unless you're willing to pay overtime rates."

"I was afraid of that." She shrugged and reached behind her for the doorknob. Why had she suddenly felt the need to confess her troubles to him? Just because he was a fix-it kind of guy didn't mean he wanted to repair what was broken in her life. "Never mind. I'll have to revert to the methods I used before I owned a dryer."

"What? Put your underwear in the microwave?" he suggested with a grin. "Drive around town with wet clothes hanging off the radio antenna? Spread the laundry over a bush?"

Now it was her turn to laugh, and the tension and embarrassment that had nearly made her sick evaporated in an instant. "I can take the wet clothes to the Laundromat."

"Sounds like a headache. Tell you what. I'll take a look at it for you. Might not be able to buy a new belt until tomorrow though."

The cinnamon fragrance *was* getting stronger. Couldn't he smell it? Maybe she'd accidentally left her near-empty cup on the "mug mate" warming plate on her desk. She'd better check it before she left for the day. She didn't want to burn the place down. "You'd do that?"

"You don't have to act so amazed." His words were affronted, but his expression was amused. "Despite rumors to the contrary, I'm not exactly the Antichrist. I do good deeds now and then. Mostly during leap years and solar eclipses."

"I'm sorry. That was rude of me. It's just that you always seem so busy."

"I stay busy for a reason. Doesn't mean I'm always on duty."

"I used to joke that I might as well live at work. You really do." He owned the building and maintained a loft apartment upstairs. Did he ever get lonely? At the end of a long day, did he ever want someone to talk to? No. Those were her feelings, and she had to stop projecting them on him. Men like Trick didn't lack for company. "Doesn't that blur the line between your professional and personal lives?"

"I like the convenience."

Like Ace, Trick had no family or personal attachments. No hobbies. No outside interests. She worked to live, but Trick was driven. He lived to work. Fighting oil well fires was more than his occupation. It was more like a religious calling. He stayed busy for a reason. Did he ever think something was missing from his life? Clearly he was more comfortable doing things than talking about feelings.

He smacked his palms down on the desk. "I have some free time this evening. Do you want me to take a look at your dryer or not?"

"Yes! Please." His words reminded her of the first night they'd met. He'd asked almost the same thing about her car. She'd been taking care of herself all her life, and yet when Trick was around, she seemed to have problems only he could fix. "I'd appreciate your help, if you're sure you don't mind."

"If I minded, I wouldn't offer. What's the address?" She gave it to him. "That's, what? Three blocks away?"

"Yes."

"Convenient." He grinned. "I'll be there at seven." It was a statement, not a suggestion.

"I'll see you then. It's after five. I should

157

probably go." Brandy ducked out of the office. Was it possible to feel terrified and exhilarated at the same time? Of course, it was. That's what made roller coasters and haunted houses so popular. Sheesh! What kind of Stepford idiot was she? In a moment of tongue-tied insanity, she had invited a man into her home. And not just any man. One who made her remember what it was like to feel. Made her want things. She should have said thanks, but no thanks and hightailed it out of there. She should have asked Ace to look at the dryer. Without even trying, Trick Templeton brought out the dumbest in her.

What was she thinking? She never behaved impulsively. A brain-mushing spell or hypnotism might explain her rash actions. Even if her imagination rivaled Chloe's, she could never picture her sexy boss tinkering around with her appliances.

When she returned to her desk, she expected to find an overheated cup of tea, but the warming plate was unplugged, the cup empty. Just as she remembered. At least she'd done something right today. With no time to ponder the strange occurrence, she grabbed her purse and drove to the after-school program for Chloe. She would worry about Trick's visit later. Right now, all she could think was, thank goodness, she'd straightened up the house on her lunch hour today.

Fifteen minutes later, Chloe settled into her booster seat and buckled her own seatbelt. "So, Mommy," she asked with barely concealed glee. "Did anything interesting happen at work today?"

Brandy smiled. Usually, she was the one who asked that question to elicit news of Chloe's activities. "Not really." She checked the seat's safety strap and steered out of the school drive. "What was interesting about your day?"

"Science. We did experiments and learned about magnetic attraction."

"That *is* interesting." Brandy had also learned a lesson in magnetic attraction today.

"If you try to make the ends of two magnets touch," Chloe went on, "they won't stick together. But if you make the sides touch, they do. You know what that proves?"

"No, what?" Brandy smiled. Chloe had the curiosity of a tiny researcher.

"Attraction won't work unless the poles are in the right place."

"Right." The innocent conversation only increased Brandy's anxiety over Trick's upcoming visit. Keeping things under control at the office was one thing. Handling that magnetism in a different place might prove difficult.

"Can we bake cookies when we get home?" Chloe's agile mind quickly shifted from one subject to another. Her grandmother had made her an apron with her name on the front and she loved helping in the kitchen. "I think we should."

"You do?" Brandy glanced in the rearview mirror before pulling into rush hour traffic and caught Chloe leaning over in the seat and nodding as though listening to a silent conversation.

"Yep."

Brandy glanced in the mirror again. Her daughter was giggling. "Maybe if I have the right ingredients. What kind of cookies do you want to make?"

"Snickerdoodles!"

Chapter Seven

An experienced soldier on a dangerous mission, Trick arrived ten minutes early and completed a thorough reconnaissance before approaching Brandy's house. A man should know what he was getting into. Located in an older neighborhood in the center of town, the 1940s bungalow had been well maintained over the years. The small gray house was a graceful old lady, hiding its age behind carefully applied cosmetics of vinyl siding, new shingles and fresh paint.

Planted and nurtured by long-gone residents, tall oaks had survived years of harsh plains temperatures and now lined the quiet evening streets like sentinels. In a few weeks, they'd dump their burden of leaves, creating extra work for homeowners. For now, before they trembled and fell, the muted fall colors provided what passed for an autumn display in west Texas.

A gentle breeze set a porch swing creaking at one end of the wide covered veranda. Clay pots of perky yellow chrysanthemums flanked the entry. Abandoned by its young rider, a small pink bicycle with training wheels leaned against the steps.

Soft light beckoned through windows hung with softly rustling lace curtains. Except for the romping puppy and white picket fence, Brandy's house was pretty much what he'd expected. Homey. Lived-in. Inviting. Everything he didn't want. At least, everything he would never admit he wanted.

He locked his truck, an unnecessary precaution in the sleepy neighborhood, and walked up the cracked sidewalk with toolbox in hand. He hesitated on the porch, suddenly eager *and* anxious. Like a first-time skydiver poised at the door of a plane, he had a pretty good idea where his next step would take him. Exhilarating fall. Painful landing.

What had prompted him to break his own rules by coming here? Plain and simple, he'd wanted to see her. He'd missed her while he was in New Mexico. Which was pretty pathetic. How could he miss something he'd never had? He hardly knew Brandy, and yet longing haunted him. Maybe what he really craved was feeling more than just alive. Of being part of something bigger. He'd always gotten that rush from fighting out-of-control fires, but for the past few months, the old thrill had not been enough. He wanted more.

Despite his foolish yearning, if she hadn't needed his help, he could not have spent time with Brandy away from the office. Over the years, he'd maintained proper employer-employee protocol at all costs. In all the time Wylodene Talbott had worked for Hotspur, he couldn't remember ever being inside her house. He knew very little about her personal life. Maybe that's why her elopement had taken him by surprise.

Policy prohibited him from socializing with his men as well. He'd set firm boundaries when he took over the company. Men in dangerous jobs had to trust their boss with their lives. He'd succeeded by making decisions with his head. Not his heart. A commanding officer who'd drawn a line he couldn't cross, Trick did not fraternize with the troops.

So what was he doing here now? Why was he tempting fate? He shifted the heavy toolbox to his other hand, but still couldn't bring himself to knock. He had to be a glutton for punishment. Brandy had obviously blurted out her appliance problem this afternoon to defuse the explosive situ-

163

ation ticking between them. Despite recent evidence to the contrary, he wasn't an idiot. He'd felt her response, body and soul. He'd used every bit of control he had to appear unaffected. It was no easy task to remain outwardly calm while being pelted by a hailstorm of awareness and desire.

His imagination, however, had run wild. His aching arms had known exactly how it would feel to hold Brandy's trembling body close. His dry mouth had tasted the sweetness of her lips opening to his probing tongue. His buzzing ears had heard her moan with pleasure and fulfill-ment. His response had not been com-pletely metaphorical. After she'd left, he'd sat in his chair for several minutes, waiting impatiently for his aroused body to return to normal.

This evening was gonna be some fun.

No worries. All he had to do was what he did best. Determine the problem with her dryer and fix it. Get in. Get out. Moving objects were hard to catch. Where women were concerned, his whole philos-ophy was based on strike-and-retreat tac-tics. Shock and awe. Never slow down long enough to step in snares.

Soft feminine laughter drifted out the open window, lilting over the familiar strains of an old rock song. Working in a coal mine. That's where he'd rather be right now. Back in the deep, dark safe hole in which he'd existed for so many years. He raised his hand and knocked.

Brandy's daughter opened the door. Little Bit wore a red butcher's apron with the words, Chloe — Mommy's Little Helper emblazoned on the front. She carried a huge spatula as regally as a queen's scepter. Her pixie face and apron were liberally dusted with sugar and cinnamon.

"Oh, goody. You're finally here," she said without preamble. "Come in, Trick. Mommy will be out in a minute. She's in the kitchen. We're baking."

"I figured." The child's round face, pointed chin, uptipped nose and bright eyes made him smile. She embodied his childhood images of pixies and elves and other wondrous folk. A small package, bursting with fun and magic.

She shut the door and ushered him into the living room. Offered him a chair. He glanced around, quickly taking in the room. Pale buttery yellow walls. Wood floor. Nondescript furniture. Comfortable, but far from new. Vanilla candles burned on the mantel over a fake fireplace. Piles of paperback courtroom novels and children's

165

picture books. A two-story plastic doll-house filled one corner. A doll here. A stuffed animal there. Framed photos on the walls and tables. Plants on the window-sill. A *Beauty and the Beast* coloring book and scattered crayons on the scratched coffee table. Unless he missed his guess, there'd be kid drawings under fruit-shaped magnets on the refrigerator door.

The house was cozy. Clean, but not overly neat. Full of welcoming fragrances and the trappings of everyday life. Unlike his sterile monk's cell of an apartment, people obviously lived here. Loved here. Laughed and cried.

He sniffed, taking in a scent of cinnamon more powerful than the candles. "Mmm. Something smells good."

"We made cookies." Chloe plopped down on an ottoman near his chair, planted elbows on knees and leaned forward with chin in hands. "You *do* love snickerdoodles, right?"

"Right. But how did you —"

"I'm sorry." Brandy walked out of the kitchen wiping her hands on a blue-checked dish towel. Trick had never seen her looking anything but professional, and his heart turned over at the transformation. Loosened from its braid, her long hair fell like dark silk over her shoulders. Faded jeans molded lithe, shapely legs. A white tank top under an open vintage blue Western shirt revealed an unexpected lushness. He'd never guessed her prim suits hid so many curves. "I was taking something out of the oven."

He jumped to his feet, and so did the child. "No problem. Chloe's a gracious hostess."

"Yes, she is." Brandy gave her daughter a quick, encouraging wink. "Please, have a seat, Mr. Templeton."

"I thought you agreed to call me Trick. Am I early?"

"No." She glanced at the clock on the mantel. "As a matter of fact, you're right on time."

"I try to do what I say." However, at the moment, he was doing the very thing he'd sworn not to do. He was getting involved. Irrational considering his life-long policy of detachment, but he wanted to be here with Brandy and Chloe instead of where he usually was. Alone.

"An admirable quality." Brandy's nervousness showed in the way she folded and refolded the dish towel. "Not everyone is so reliable these days." Apparently, she had personal experience with unreliable men. Chloe's father, most likely.

The smiling child stood between him and her mother, short blond hair swinging as she raptly followed the adult conversation. She was interested, almost as if she had a stake in its outcome.

"You brought your tools." Brandy indicated the black metal box at his feet. "If you're in a hurry, would you like to take a look at the dryer now?"

"Good idea." Time to get back on track. Lord, in a moment of weakness, he'd almost surrendered to the sweet, sheltering warmth of the little house. Funny how unexpected yearning could overpower reason. He'd taken one look at Brandy and wondered how it would feel to come home to a family instead of a cold, empty room. To know what he was fighting for when he battled raging fires. How unlike him to get so caught up in wishful speculation that he'd almost forgotten why he was here.

Picking up his tools, Trick followed Brandy to the back of the house. Chloe skipped at his side. They passed through a large eat-in kitchen, also painted yellow, but more lemon than butter. He grinned at the anticipated gallery of childish drawings on the fridge. On the aging counter, wire racks held neat rows of cooling cinnamon-dusted cookies. His mouth watered, and he was hit by powerful memories of helping his grandmother on baking day. Like Chloe, he'd been allowed to roll the balls of shortbread dough in cinnamon and sugar before placing them on baking sheets.

"Would you like some lemonade and a cookie before you start, Trick?" Little Miss Manners asked.

"Maybe when I'm done." He needed to finish the job and make his escape before the emotional hole he seemed to be digging for himself got any deeper.

Brandy opened the door leading out to the attached garage. "The washer and dryer are out here."

He surveyed the setup. The dryer had a top-mounted lint screen. "This shouldn't take long."

"I'll leave you to your work then." Brandy stepped back into the kitchen. "Just let me know if you need anything."

"Can I stay and watch?" Chloe asked.

"Why don't you come in and put the cookies in the jar for me?" Brandy suggested gently. "You might get in Trick's way."

Chloe's shoulders drooped in disappointment. He spoke up. "She won't be in my way. Besides, I might need a helper." He smiled at the child. "Do you want to hand me the tools I need?"

Her eyes brightened and the sun rose in her little face. Was it really that easy to make a child happy?

Brandy gave him a grateful smile. She started to close the door and then stopped as though a thought had just occurred to her. "We're just having hamburgers for supper, but if you haven't eaten, you're welcome to stay."

Before he could automatically refuse the invitation, Chloe grasped her hands together in front of her heart in a pleading gesture. "Please, please stay, Trick," she wheedled. "Mommy makes really good burgers."

He'd already jumped out of the plane by coming here. Might as well enjoy the scenery during his free fall. "Sure. Why not?"

"Take Celestian with you," Chloe directed her mother. "He *will* get in the way."

"Right. We'll eat when you're done then." Brandy went inside and closed the door.

"So who's this Celestian I hear you talking about?" Trick asked.

"He's my friend." Chloe sighed. "Before you ask, yes, he's real and no, you can't see him. Only I can."

"So he's imaginary?"

"Nope. Imaginary means not real. Mommy said. He says he was sent here to help me, but other kids don't understand about him. He can't go to school with me anymore because they tease me about him."

"They're probably just jealous because they don't have a special friend." Another blast from the past. His grandmother had told him the same thing about his imaginary playmate.

"So you understand about Celestian?" she asked hopefully.

"Sure I do. I used to have an invisible dragon for a pet."

"You did?" Her dark eyes widened in surprise. "For real?"

"Billy was real to me." He hadn't thought about his childhood companion for years. His parents were away from him for long stretches, and he'd taken comfort in an imaginary dragon that stuck close to his side. Though pragmatic in most things, his intuitive grandmother had accepted Billy's presence. She'd understood that Trick needed the comfort of having a companion who would never leave him. Later, when he'd begged to join his father's crew, she'd cautioned him that fighting demon

171

fires was harder than slaying dragons.

"So where is Billy now?" Chloe asked.

"I don't know. One day, he wasn't there anymore." Like the rest of Trick's illusions, Billy had disappeared shortly after his mother's death.

"When you grew up, he prolly found another kid to live with," Chloe suggested.

"I'll bet you're right. How'd you get so smart?"

She shrugged. "Grandpa says I'm too smart for my own good."

"Nah. There's no such thing as being too smart. Hey, we'd better get busy, or we won't finish the job before supper." Trick banished thoughts of the past. Concentrating on the present was the best way to avoid thinking about the future, too.

"So what do we do first?" Chloe hunkered down on the concrete floor beside him. He opened his toolbox.

"First we unplug the dryer."

"So we don't get a shock, right?"

"Right. Hand me that screwdriver. The one with the yellow handle." Chloe performed her assignment with the gravity of an operating room assistant placing a scalpel in a surgeon's hand. He removed the screws holding the top on the dryer. "Do you know what a putty knife is?"

"Is it to cut Silly Putty?"

"Not exactly." He removed the tool from the tray. "I'm going to use it to pry off the top and toe panel."

"Good idea. What's a toe panel?" He explained, and she hovered over his shoulder, seemingly fascinated by his every action and word. She smelled like sunshine and cookies, warm and sweet. "You're really smart about dryers," she said with genuine admiration.

He wouldn't tell her that compared to the machinery he usually worked with, this task was a no-brainer. The job would go a lot faster if Chloe wasn't asking so many questions, but he'd never been anyone's hero before.

In the kitchen, Brandy adjusted the heat under the frying pan and turned the ground beef patties. She still wasn't sure why she'd invited Trick to stay for dinner. She certainly hadn't planned to, but couldn't seem to control her impulses around him. She set the table and tossed a salad. Sliced raw carrots for Chloe who considered lettuce "slimy." Surely a man like Trick had better things to do on a Friday night than eat homemade burgers with his office manager. That's all she was to him, and she'd be smart to remember

173

that important piece of information.

Barely twenty minutes later, the door to the garage opened. Chloe bounced in first, full of excitement. She loved learning new things, and it had been a long time since she'd seemed so happy. "Guess what, Mommy?"

"What?" Brandy set glasses on the table. Milk for Chloe, lemonade for the adults.

"Trick said I can be his helper anytime." Chloe bubbled with excitement. "Can't I, Trick?"

"You sure can. You're a natural. Didn't take you long at all to learn the difference between a Phillips head and a regular screwdriver."

Brandy smiled to let Trick know how grateful she was for the praise he lavished on Chloe.

"So did you two master mechanics get that old fossil running again?"

"Yep!" Chloe beamed. "It stopped working because the . . . uh . . . what's that part called again, Trick?"

"Drive belt," he supplied helpfully.

"Right. The drive belt was off. That old hunk of junk is working like a dream now."

Brandy smiled again. Obviously, Chloe was quoting Trick. "What a relief. Why don't you run and wash up for supper?

We'll be eating in a minute."

After Chloe left, Brandy offered Trick the sink and a bar of soap. "You can clean up here, if you want." While he scrubbed his hands, she finished putting food on the table. "Why was the dryer making that racket this week?"

"It was rocking. All I had to do was adjust the leveling feet. I expected the drive belt to be broken, but it seems fine. I just had to loop the belt under the idler pulley and catch it on the motor pulley. It should work fine now."

"That's a little more than I needed to know," she said with a laugh. "I appreciate your help. A hamburger is hardly adequate repayment, but —"

"You don't owe me a thing," he said quickly, as if to remind her no obligations linked them.

Chloe returned and asked if she could say the blessing before they ate.

"Make a circle," she commanded. Since she was seated between the adults, the arrangement forced Brandy to reach across the table to take Trick's large hand in hers. This time when they touched, instead of the powerful jolt of awareness she'd felt in the past, she was filled with an uncommon sense of peace. For a fleeting moment before she bowed her head, she thought she glimpsed the same peace in Trick's dark eyes.

"God, we thank you for this food," Chloe intoned in a high, clear voice. "For rest and home and all things good. For wind and rain and sun above. But most of all for those we love. Amen."

Brandy's heart skittered at the word love. Whispering her own amen, she wasn't sure which sentiment she agreed with. How foolhardy to even think about such things where Trick was concerned. So why did touching him feel so . . . right? She withdrew her hand from his at the end of grace, but the comforting heat lingered. There was something perfect about him being here, literally completing the circle that had been broken long before Joe left.

A breathless sense of destiny replaced her desire for food, filling her in turn with another basic human desire. Chloe chattered away, oblivious to the crackling electricity sparking between her mother and her new friend. Brandy met Trick's gaze across the table. Here, within the walls of her small house, he seemed different from the aloof employer she encountered at the office. Here he seemed . . . familiar.

As illogical as it seemed, she knew this

man. Her body was well acquainted with his. In the weeks since they'd met, she'd tried to ignore the fateful, whispery feelings, but she could not deny them in their present context. He *was* here for a reason. Her mind might refuse to recognize a connection with Trick Templeton, but her hungry heart could not.

For once, the man who was always on the move seemed in no hurry to leave. Brandy didn't know what to make of this, so after dinner, she busied herself stacking dishes in the sink. Every time she glanced at Trick, she found him watching her. Not in a creepy, gauging-her-every-move, judgmental way. He looked at her like someone who'd made a startling discovery he wasn't quite convinced was real.

He sat at the table with Chloe, talking and munching cookies, but Brandy couldn't shake the feeling that if her daughter weren't present, conversation would be the last thing on his mind. A flush of desire burned its way up her neck, and she went to the refrigerator for the lemonade pitcher, hoping the cold interior would cool her off before Trick noticed.

"You should go into the cookie business, Little Bit," Trick said as Brandy refilled his glass. "These are the best cookies I ever tasted."

"Even better than your grandma's?" she teased.

He laughed, but was obviously taken aback by the question. "What? Are you a mind reader too? How'd you know my granny used to make snickerdoodles?"

"You told me." She casually reached for another cookie.

"I don't think so."

"You must have." She coyly fluttered her eyelashes at him. "How else would I know?"

Brandy watched the exchange and smiled. No one could express complete innocence like an ingenuous five-year-old. Especially *her* ingenuous five-year-old. Brandy packed cookies into a small tin, which she set on the table beside him. "I know it isn't much, but please take these home with you as a token of our appreciation."

"Thanks." He picked up the tin and pushed to his feet. His gaze met and held hers, a little longer than was comfortable. "I should be going. I don't think the dryer will give you any more trouble for a while, but if it does, just let me know. I guarantee my work."

"Thank you again." She flipped on the

porch light. Holding Chloe's hand, she followed him outside.

"Do you have to leave, Trick?" Chloe hated to see a good thing end. So did Brandy, but she wasn't about to let him know she wanted him to stay as much as her little girl did.

"I really do. Besides, isn't it about your bedtime?" He stood on the sidewalk in the evening gloom, his toolbox in one hand and the tin of cookies in the other. A cricket chirped under the hydrangea bush next to the porch. Overhead, stars blinked to life.

"I don't know. Is there school tomorrow?" she asked Brandy.

"Tomorrow's Saturday, sweetie."

"Then I can stay up till eight thirty," she announced triumphantly.

Trick leaned down and whispered conspiratorially. "Sorry, kiddo, it's already past that."

"Oh." Chloe looked crestfallen, but bounced back with childish resilience. "If tomorrow is Saturday, it's dancing day, right Mommy?"

"Right."

"Is it Daddy day, too?"

"Not this week." Brandy explained that on Joe's designated visitation weekends, he

179

accompanied Chloe to dance class before taking her to his home in Slapdown.

"Will you come and watch me dance, Trick? Pretty please. I can do heel-toe now."

"I don't know, pixie-face. In my line of work, I can't plan too far ahead."

"But you will come, if you can, right? Mommy, tell him where the dance place is."

Brandy gave him the address to Miss Robin's studio as well as the time Chloe's class started. She lifted an apologetic shoulder to tell him he wasn't really expected to appear.

"Can I give you a baby bear hug before you leave?" Chloe asked Trick.

He looked to Brandy, and she nodded her permission. At that moment, she envied her child. He knelt on one knee so Chloe could wrap her thin arms around his neck, and Brandy longed to do the same. She wanted to test the feelings he aroused in her. See if they were as real as they seemed.

She couldn't hear what Chloe whispered in his ear, but her words made his eyes widen. He bid them good night and nearly ran to his truck.

"So what did you tell Trick just now?" Brandy asked casually as they watched him drive away.

"I told him I was glad he came tonight."

"That was nice."

"I told him he's just what we need."

"Chloe! Why would you say something like that?" Brandy was dismayed by her daughter's honesty. She might want a physical relationship with Trick Templeton, but that was definitely not what she needed. She hoped he knew enough about children not to take the comment seriously.

"It's true!" Chloe protested. "He *is* what we need. And we're just what he needs, too. Don't you think we feel like a family when he's here?"

Hand in hand, they strolled inside, and Brandy shut and locked the front door. She tugged Chloe onto the couch beside her. "Honey. You and I *are* a family. And you have Daddy and Mallory. You're such a lucky little girl, you have *two* families."

"I know. But Trick doesn't have even one. I think he's lonely."

"Yes, baby, I think so, too." She'd probably mistaken loneliness for attraction tonight. Stood to reason. He wasn't interested in her. Just grateful for the home-cooked meal. She'd read too much into those long looks, but Chloe saw the truth with a child's unclouded vision. Distracted by physical attraction, Brandy had missed the obvious. Trick *was* lonely. He used gruffness to hide his pain. He wasn't at all short or demanding tonight. Chloe brought out the best in him. He'd seemed like a different person, but in reality she had finally seen a different side of him. That's all.

Brandy wanted to deny the strange circumstances that had crossed her path with his, but after tonight, the fatefulness of their meeting could not be ignored. Now that she'd seen a gentler side of him, she began to wonder if maybe Trick *could* be what she needed as well as what she wanted. It was possible that she'd landed the job at Hotspur for a more important reason than money. Maybe meeting Trick was more than the answer to *her* prayer.

Dare she hope that she and Chloe might be the answer to his?

"Do you ever get lonely, Mommy?" Chloe climbed into her lap.

Brandy held her close and kissed her hair. "How could I ever be lonely? I have you. You know how you like to leave the night light on at night so you can see?"

"Yes."

"Well, you're my light in the darkness." Although Chloe had a vivid imagination, she helped Brandy see what was real.

"Like a candle?" she whispered.

"Exactly like a candle."

"But I'm a little candle."

"You may be little, but you're bright." Brandy blinked away tears. Maybe Trick wasn't the one. Maybe she was destined to spend the rest of her life without a man. It didn't matter. She would never be alone.

"Are you sad, Mommy?"

Brandy couldn't deny a certain wistfulness that made her wish for a fuller life. One that included someone who would complete her as Trick had completed the circle at dinner. She'd never objected to carrying her own load, but the thought of sharing it was appealing. She was tired of being alone. She was ready to face the truth.

She wanted a husband. A partner. A full-time father for Chloe. More children. She wanted to feel someone breathing gently beside her in the dark, and know he would shield her from life's storms. Since her divorce, she'd never even come close. Hadn't really dated or looked. She'd worked at independence to prove something to herself. Now she knew. Now she was ready.

Acknowledging her deepest desire made her next words ring with truth. "No, baby, I'm not sad. I'm happy."

"Me, too." Chloe yawned. "Celestian says Trick will make us happy. I didn't know what he meant before. But now I do."

Brandy hugged her daughter. Since Celestian always seemed to be in the middle of things, he was probably a safe, outward expression of Chloe's internal needs. Maybe filtering her interest in Trick through her imagination allowed her to better understand it. That made sense. As a teen, Brandy had written down her fondest hopes and dreams in a diary. Not so different from confiding in an invisible friend.

H.A.R.P. Field Report
From: Celestian, Earthbound Operative
To: Mission Control
Re: Operation True Love

Current Objective: Male and Female subjects will spend minimum of two hours together in nonthreatening setting outside mutual workplace.

Progress Notes: Objective met. Male subject demonstrates new level of positive emotional growth by responding favorably to female subject's overt nurturing skills.

Female subject demonstrates marked decrease in opposition to potential relationship by recognizing male subject's use of external distancing behaviors to conceal intrinsic vulnerability.

Successful management of environmental manipulation and emotional retraining to date indicate the acceleration of therapeutic methods now viable.

Plan: Establish new goals to increase subjects' emotional dependency and obtain baseline measurement of physical compatibility.

Chapter Eight

Trick planned to sleep in the next morning, but old habits died hard, and he was up at 6:00 a.m. Alert and ready to start the day. He never set an alarm. He went to bed, told himself when to awake and depended on his internal timekeeper to do the rest. Big mistake.

He'd spent a restless night tossing and turning and punching his pillow. Like a hormonal teenager, he'd replayed every moment spent with Brandy in her cozy little cookie jar of a house. Rewound every snippet of conversation. He couldn't stop thinking about her. She was a melody stuck in his brain, and when he finally fell into fitful sleep, her dark eyes and gentle smile haunted his dreams.

He wouldn't mope around mooning all day. The best cure for an itch he couldn't scratch was to get busy and stay that way.

Clad only in boxers, Trick sat on the edge of the bed with his cell phone and checked for messages. Nothing. He listened to his company voice mail. Nada.

Just his luck. When he needed to refocus his attention on work, there wasn't a single oil well fire in the whole wide world for him to fight. What were the odds of that? The crew would be happy. They'd returned from New Mexico tired and ready for a break. Eager to be with their families. Glad for a chance to maintain equipment and restock supplies. They worked hard and appreciated every opportunity to rest and regroup.

As much as the men treasured downtime, Trick hated it. He never knew what to do when he wasn't working. How many times had Wylo suggested he take up a hobby? Phrased in her succinct way, the admonition was more like, get a life. And when she was feeling salty, get a *damn* life!

Normally, he used the lull between jobs to drum up new business. Track industry trends. Research the latest in firefighting technology. Well control wasn't all fireworks and technique. Politics played a role too. He had to work the good-old-boy network, meet with petroleum engineers and CEOs of oil companies. Get the word out about what Hotspur could do for them. He glanced at the date on his watch. Oh, yeah. He hated weekends, too. No business until Monday.

He could run downstairs to catch up on work in his office, but since Brandy had taken over, there was nothing to catch up *on*. She was a wizard of organization. As her employer, he should admire her work ethic, competence and reliability. Her dedication to the job. Even her punctuality. If he were willing to be a jerk, which he wasn't where she was concerned, he could justify admiring her shapely figure and pretty face. At least chauvinism was a category of male behavior he understood.

He threw the down comforter over the bed and padded into the bathroom. The feelings Brandy aroused in him were far from simple. Instead of satisfying his curiosity, being with her last night had only whetted his appetite. He wanted more. He wanted to get to know her, to find out who she was and what made her tick. He wanted to learn about the little things. What music did she listen to in the car? Did she prefer corn or flour tortillas in her enchiladas? Baths or showers? Chocolate or vanilla? He wanted to know about the big things too. What were her goals? Her guiding principles? What made her happy? What made her cry?

That was a whole new kind of desire for him. He'd never wanted to get to *know* a woman before. At least in any sense other than purely biblical. His inexplicable attraction to Brandy was uncharted territory, but she made him willing to stumble into the emotional frontier without a map. For the first time in his life, he wanted to see where the involvement path might lead.

Now why didn't that scare the hell out of him?

He pondered that question while brushing his teeth. The problem was simple. He was thirty-seven years old and had never been in love. He'd never met a woman he thought he *could* love, at least not forever. Or for any longer than right now. Brandy must have tripped the detonator on some weird male biological clock. Memory snagged the image of her standing on the porch last night with Chloe, waving goodbye. He suddenly wanted to know what it would be like to leave a real home every day, knowing a real woman like Brandy was waiting for his return. He wanted someone to miss him. To think about him in his absence. Wasn't that the difference between living and existing?

Or was it love?

Whoa, cowboy. Love. Talk about making a premature mountain out of an unlikely molehill. Going from zero to sixty a little

189

too fast. He wouldn't know if Brandy was meant to fill the empty spaces in his life until he understood what, if anything, was missing.

Barefoot and bare-chested, Trick surveyed the contents of his hi-tech refrigerator. Orange juice, a shriveled lime, some kind of unnaturally green cheese and a bottle of Tabasco sauce. Only the OJ hadn't passed its expiration date, so he leaned against the counter and drank from the carton. Where was that elusive cinnamon scent coming from? Looking around, he spied the tin Brandy had sent home with him and smiled. Right. Cookies. The way to a man's heart was through his gastric system. He ate one, then another. The sweets eased his hunger, but focused his thoughts more firmly on the woman who'd made them.

It was counterproductive to think about Brandy like this. He couldn't date his office manager. Doing so went against the company policy he'd established as well as personal principles. The situation was complicated by the fact that she kept a tight, almost desperate, lid on her own emotions. Last night, she'd been gracious, but nervous and aloof, looking away whenever their eyes met. She'd hosted an impromptu supper for the boss who'd

190

repaired her ailing appliance. Nobody had crossed any lines. She'd given him no indication of being open to a relationship outside the office.

Really, Templeton. I know you're dense, but are you deaf and blind too? Does a house have to drop on you?

The thought echoed through the silent apartment like a spoken rebuke. It seemed so real, Trick swung around and checked for intruders. The sterile, underfurnished apartment was empty. No one here but us chickens, as Granny Bett used to say. He laughed uneasily. Sleep deprivation played hell with a man's concentration and it obviously caused auditory hallucinations. Imagination was running away with him again. He was alone.

What else was new?

Growing older had taught him one thing. Solitude was *not* all it was cracked up to be. Meeting Brandy made him forget why he thought batching it was so much fun. He'd spent more than fifteen years building walls against anyone who threatened his single status. The way things were going, he might spend the rest of his life lamenting his success.

That's what you get for being so darned good at everything.

Needing the liberation of physical activity, Trick pulled on sweats and took a long run through the nearly empty morning streets. It had rained in the night, filling gutters and washing the world clean. If only he could wipe out his preoccupation with Brandy so easily. Returning home, he showered and dressed. Read a trade journal. Switched on the TV and flipped through news channels. Sorted a pile of mail. Waited for something to demand his immediate attention. Checked his watch. Barely nine o'clock. His exasperated groan made him recall something else.

Granny Bett had always said there were two kinds of people in the world. Those who woke up and said, "Good morning, Lord," and those who woke up and said, "Good Lord, it's morning." She'd spoiled her solemn delivery by tickling his ribs and asking him what he was going to be that day.

Greeter or groaner?

Bettina Templeton had been a wise woman. After five years, he still missed her. At eighty, she'd suffered a stroke during another rare lull in his busy schedule. He had hurried to Missouri, reaching the Springfield hospital shortly before she slipped away. Unable to talk, she had squeezed his hand when he whispered his love for her.

Who would be there when he breathed his last? Who would hold his hand? Who would tell him he was loved when he departed this earth?

Granny Bett had been his last human connection. He'd avoided commitment by rejecting people before they could get too close. He'd achieved his objective. He was alone. Had he been wrong all along? Brandy and Chloe made him think. Meaning something to others might be what made life worth living. Another gust of cinnamon scent sent him back to the cookie tin.

Took you long enough. Get off your arse and get out there, man. Connect already.

Trick was filled with new resolve. He'd groaned enough for one day. It wasn't too late. He could still make it to Chloe's dance class. He pushed to his feet. It might be just what he needed. A refreshing change of pace. A diversion. A legitimate excuse to see Brandy again.

About time! Best idea you've had in ages.

Trick switched off the light and locked the door. He ran down the iron steps outside with a determined bounce in his step. He couldn't agree more.

★ ★ ★

The Back Stage Dance Studio was located in a strip mall between a pet grooming shop and a video store. Chattering five-year-olds and their parents filled the small reception area, waiting for the next class to begin.

Brandy took a seat, but Chloe stood near the front, gazing out. "He might not come." She had to prepare her daughter for disappointment.

"He'll be here." Chloe stared out the plate-glass window. She'd kept the parking lot under constant surveillance since they arrived a few minutes ago.

"I know you want him to come. But he may have to work."

"Nope, he doesn't." Dressed in pink tights, a black leotard and patent leather tap shoes tied with black ribbon bows, Chloe turned away from the window and settled on the bench beside her. "Trick doesn't have any work to do today."

"How do you know that?"

"Celestian said."

"Honey, Celestian might not know everything about Trick's schedule."

Chloe laughed. "Yes, he does. That's his job. Celestian says Trick will come to see us. He 'zagerates, but he doesn't lie."

194

Brandy smiled. "But just in case Trick can't make it —"

"There he is!" Chloe jumped off the bench, bolted to the window and pressed her face against the glass. "I told you! See?"

She did. Brandy watched a white truck with the Hotspur logo on the door pull into a parking space. Trick climbed out and pointed a keyless entry device to lock the door. He strode purposefully toward the building, his long legs clad in knife-pleated khakis. His electric blue, long-sleeved shirt created an eye-catching display of shoulders. Polished loafers replaced the usual boots. He wasn't wearing the cowboy hat, and wind tousled his dark hair. He reached up and smoothed it straight back from his tanned forehead. In his other hand, he carried a single long-stemmed pink rosebud wrapped in a sheath of green tissue paper.

When he entered the dance studio, an involuntary collective "ah" arose from the other mothers. Brandy didn't blame them. Trick Templeton was a sigh-out-loud kind of guy. He approached, and her stomach lurched with anticipation.

"I must be in the right place." Chloe's head bobbed enthusiastically in the affirmative, and he handed her the rose.

"For me?" she gasped.

"All dancing divas need flowers."

"Nobody ever gave me a real rose before."

Trick grinned. "It may be your first, Little Bit, but it won't be your last."

"What do you say, Chloe?" Brandy prompted.

"Thank you, Trick. I'll dance my best for you. I'm glad you're here."

He responded to Chloe, but his gaze focused on Brandy. "Me, too."

Before she could reply, the door to the dance room flew open and twelve tiny ballerinas and their parents filed out. Miss Robin greeted Chloe's class, and the children's taps pattered the floor like a miniature hailstorm as they rushed to their assigned places. Chloe relinquished the rose to Brandy, who led Trick to a section of stadium-style seats reserved for observers. He settled on the bench beside her. Close. Maybe a little too close. She could smell the soap he'd used this morning and feel the heat emanating from his big body.

When the music started, Trick leaned in and spoke softly. "You seem surprised to see me. I *was* invited."

Heady awareness rocketed through

Brandy, warming her from the inside out. She had to be crazy to feel so happy. To be so grateful for so little. She'd rehearsed what she'd say if he showed up today, but now that he was here, her mind went blank. So she went with the truth. "I'm glad you came."

His dark gaze held hers. "You are?"

"Of course. For Chloe's sake," she clarified. "She was so sure you'd show up. Thank you for not disappointing her."

Chloe caught Trick's eye from the dance floor. Beaming, she held her hand close to her chest and gave him a surreptitious wave. He waved back. "I wanted to come. You probably won't understand this, because I don't. But I woke up this morning knowing I had to be here."

Brandy swallowed hard. She had no idea how to respond to such an unexpected confession. Did he feel the powerful attraction buzzing between them, or was she imagining things again? Confused and exhilarated, she focused her attention on her daughter, whose dancing was, indeed, inspired.

When the class was over, Trick waited outside the ladies' room while Brandy helped Chloe change into street clothes. Chloe held their hands as they walked across the parking lot, creating a conduit for the unspoken need that flowed between them.

They hadn't talked much during the forty-minute class. Studio etiquette prohibited conversation that distracted the children. Brandy had given the illusion of paying rapt attention as Chloe mastered step-ball-change, but in reality, she had been unable to think about anything except Trick's words.

I woke up this morning knowing I had to be here.

It was pretty hard to deny a pervasive sense of destiny where he was concerned. Was it possible they were part of a plan neither of them understood? If he felt something, too, maybe the feeling was real. She knew better than to get her hopes up too high. Recent strange occurrences might have tipped her off normal-center, making her read too much into his remark.

"Trick, you wanna go to Mister Cheesie's with us?" Chloe chirped.

Brandy was about to provide him with an excuse, but stopped. She needed to know what would happen if she didn't give him an easy way out. "We usually have lunch after class. If you like pizza and singing mechanical mice, you're welcome to join us."

"Will you, Trick?" Chloe asked. "Please!"

"I don't know about the mice," he said with a grin, "but I love pizza."

"With barbecue chicken on top, right?"

He grinned. "How'd you know that?"

Chloe's shrug was evasive. "You told me, I guess."

Suspicion pulled his brows together. "When?"

"Once. A long time ago. You probably forgot."

Brandy buckled Chloe's booster seat before pulling out of the parking lot. Trick followed in his truck.

"I know. I didn't mean to. I'll be careful," Chloe muttered in the back.

"What did you say, baby?" Brandy asked.

"Nothing, Mommy. I was just talking to Celestian."

"I didn't think Celestian came with us today." Chloe hadn't mentioned her invisible friend all morning.

"He didn't. He came with Trick. After we eat, can I ride the helicopter and the mouse car and play the ball game too?"

"We'll see." Brandy negotiated Saturday traffic.

"Okay!" Chloe whispered fiercely. "I'll ask her."

"Ask me what?" Brandy glanced in the rearview mirror. Her daughter was engaged in another one-sided conversation. Celestian was becoming a pain. At Chloe's next checkup, she'd ask the pediatrician how to handle the situation.

"Mommy, do you like Trick?"

"I like most people, you know that."

"But do you like Trick *more* than most people?"

"I don't know him that well."

"Do you think Trick is a . . ." Chloe paused as though remembering an unfamiliar phrase, then pronounced carefully, "A prime example of virile manhood?"

"Chloe!"

"Well, do you?" she asked innocently.

"That's not a subject I'm willing to discuss with you, young lady." She used her firm, mother voice but was hard-pressed not to smile. Chloe was only five. What kind of tough questions would she be asking in ten years?

"What's virile mean?"

"Uh, strong."

"Okay, Trick's strong. If you had the chance, would you kiss him?"

"Chloe! Please don't talk about such things. Especially not in front of Trick. Do you understand?"

"Yes, ma'am," she said obediently. Then she whispered, "I think she would."

Little pitchers had big ears, and the house was small. Chloe must have overheard one of the nighttime dramas Brandy watched after tucking Chloe in bed. She would be more careful with the volume from now on.

She pulled into the restaurant's crowded parking lot and climbed out of the car. At her side, Chloe bounced with excitement as Trick approached from his truck.

A prime example of virile manhood.

Oh, Lord. That was putting it mildly.

Inside, they ordered food and drinks at the counter. Trick insisted on paying, which only increased Brandy's anxiety. The impromptu lunch had been Chloe's idea. She didn't want it to turn into a "date." Or maybe she did. That might be the problem. Chloe led them to a booth near the stage. The "Legendary Mouse Revue" was scheduled to begin in a few minutes.

Fat chance Trick would get the wrong idea and mistake this rowdy excursion for a date. With several birthday parties in full swing, the popular restaurant was packed with excited children. They ran about unattended, clutching tokens for rides and games whose unremitting clanging, ringing, tooting, buzzing and shrieking only added to the cacophony.

She smiled across the table at a bewildered Trick. "You've never been to Mister Cheesie's on Saturday, have you?"

"I've never been here on any day." He grimaced. "Can't imagine why I've deprived myself, though. Guess I never realized what I was missing. Is it always so . . . boisterous?"

"Not always." She raised her voice. "Sometimes it's really noisy."

He winced. "The decibel level in here probably exceeds OSHA safety standards."

"We can get the pizza and go if you want."

"No, no," he said. "I'm sure once my ear drums burst, I'll be fine."

Over the next hour, they watched the singing mice show twice, ate most of a large pizza and fed tokens into games and rides so Chloe could have, as Trick phrased it when buying another batch of plastic coins, "the ultimate Mr. Cheesie experience." He turned out to be an excellent skeeball player, racking up a score that made the game spit out a long strip of tickets. He handed them to Chloe and accompanied her to the redemption counter to pick out a prize.

"So what did you get?" Brandy asked when they returned.

Chloe held up a small, hot pink stuffed dragon with a red felt tongue and sleepy green eyes. "I'm going to name my new dragon Billy." She looked up at Trick, and they laughed as though sharing a secret to which she was not privy.

"Do you have plans for the rest of the afternoon?" Trick asked casually as they walked to the parking lot later.

Before Brandy could reply, Chloe announced, "We always go to the park. Wanna come?"

"It's quiet there, right?" he teased. "Just trees and squirrels and birds. No trombone-playing mice?" When Chloe nodded and laughed, he turned to Brandy. "I'd like to tag along. If I wouldn't be intruding."

The look in his eyes told Brandy he didn't want to say goodbye, either. "Not at all." Instead of nervous uncertainty, Brandy felt a sense of . . . there was that word again. Destiny. As though her life was following a secret schedule outside her control. Being with Trick felt so right that somewhere, someone was marking off the day on a big list of fateful to-dos.

Brandy Mitchum will spend a warm autumn Saturday afternoon with Trick Templeton in the park. Check!

Thrilled by the thought, she couldn't wait to see what the next item on the agenda would be.

"Do you want to ride with us?" she asked. "Or take your truck?"

"I'll follow," he said softly as he held the car door for her. "Anywhere you lead."

The adults shared a park bench in the shade while Chloe played on the equipment with her toy dragon. When she spotted a small, sniffling boy digging idly in the sandpit, she talked to him for a moment before making her report.

"That's Dillon. He's four. He's sad because he doesn't have anyone to play with. I'll be his friend, and he'll feel better." She dashed back to the sandpit, collected her new friend and the two children climbed to the top of the jungle gym tower.

"Chloe is an amazing little girl." Trick had no idea small children could be so interesting. "She's like a wise old woman in a munchkin body."

Brandy laughed. "That's one way to put it."

"Does she have a good relationship with her father?"

"She does now. Joe wasn't around much the first three years of her life. He was troubled by his father's death. Depressed and on a path of self-destruction. No matter how much I tried, I couldn't get through to him. I had to leave him. Self-preservation. Keeping Chloe and myself afloat was all I could manage."

"What changed?"

"Believe it or not, he had a near-death experience. He was struck by lightning and is a completely different person now. He was shiftless before and now he's the sheriff, a pillar of the community. He's married to the town doctor. They just built a beautiful new home in Slapdown. Chloe spends alternate weekends there."

He was hardheaded, but it wouldn't take a bolt from the blue to get through to him. He recognized a good thing when he saw it. Brandy Mitchum was a very good thing. He wanted to learn as much as he could about this gentle woman who touched him in ways no one ever had. "Tell me about your family."

"Mom and Dad live outside Midland, and we visit often. Ace told me you lost

205

both your parents. That's rough."

"It was a long time ago." He explained that his grandmother had looked after him when he was young. "This probably sounds weird, but Chloe reminds me of her. Granny Bett was a free-spirited child in an old lady's body."

Chloe raced up, and they didn't get to finish their talk. Conversation might not be what they needed. Maybe when two people were trying to learn how not to be alone, just being with someone else was enough.

Trick followed Brandy home and waited on the couch in the living room while she put a sleepy Chloe down in the bedroom.

"She was wiped out," Brandy said when she returned. "She gave up afternoon naps last year." Instead of moving the toys piled in the armchair, she sat at the opposite end of the couch.

Close enough to touch. Near enough to kiss.

Trick ignored the wayward thought. Things were going well. They'd talked. Shared glimpses of their pasts. Connected. It felt good. Right. All he had to do was go nice and slow. "She had too much fun, I guess."

"Maybe," she agreed. "I know I had a considerable amount of fun today."

"Me, too."

"Yeah? Because you don't really seem

206

like the Mister Cheesie type."

"Hey, I'm as cheesy as the next guy." He laughed. "Wait. That didn't come out right, did it?"

"You made a little girl very happy today."

"What about the big girl? Did I do anything for her?"

"You made her feel alive again." Her gaze caught his. Held it. "For the first time in years."

"You know what they say about pizza being an aphrodisiac."

She smiled. "No, I think it was the big rat. Giant rodents in top hats have always been a turn-on for me." She laughed, and in one graceful move, Trick closed the space between them.

He slid an arm around her and pulled her close. He stroked her cheek with his fingertip. "If I'm crossing a line you don't want me to cross, Brandy, now's the time to say so."

"I'll take the fifth amendment," she murmured as she found his lips.

In the first moment of their first kiss, Trick found so much more. He found answers. He found the future and the past. He found out what was missing from his life.

Chapter Nine

Brandy trembled when Trick's arms tightened around her. She pressed a palm against his chest, and the hammering beat of his heart spoke to her. Reassured her. She wasn't imagining the incredible chemistry that fired her blood and stirred her soul. He felt it, too.

They slipped into a rhythm so familiar it was as though they'd already shared a lifetime of caresses. There was no hesitation in his touch. His hands skimmed her body, lingering in the dips and hollows of her curves. Slow and deliberate. Knowing. There was no tenuous searching in his kiss. Her lips parted, and his tongue slid deep and sure into her mouth. He kissed her like a man who had finally found his way home, and she was the door he couldn't wait to open.

Instinctively he knew when to coax, when to retreat, when to renew his tender assault on her senses. Her defenses weakened. She wasn't shocked by the eagerness of her hungry response, she was delighted.

She'd been wrong. Mind-numbing desire didn't exist only in the pages of novels. Nor was it the product of an overworked imagination.

It was real. *This* was real.

For the first time in her life, Brandy understood the true meaning of passion. Breaking their languid kiss and drawing in a deep breath, Trick eased her gently back on the couch. He followed her down, and she felt the shape of him pressed upon her. *Remembered* it. Nothing in her limited sexual experience could have prepared her for so much wanting. She sighed with sudden, heady knowledge. She knew what this man would feel like inside her. She knew he could give her the release she hadn't found during the brief, unhappy days of her marriage. Trick would give her everything. He would complete her.

Such certainty should have empowered her. Instead it terrified and overwhelmed. What was going on? Need had blasted away reason. One kiss and she was ready to take a chance. To make the leap she'd resisted for years, with a man she didn't know well enough to trust. She could not allow that to happen. Never again.

"Trick," she whispered as he trailed hot kisses down her neck. "Stop. We can't do this. Not here. And not now."

He froze, hesitating only a moment before sitting up. His breathing was ragged as he pulled her close and wrapped his arms around her. "You're right." Was that relief in his voice? "We can't. Wrong place *and* wrong time." He smoothed a strand of hair off her face and trailed a fingertip along her jaw. "I could make excuses and say I got a little carried away, but that would be a lie. I got a *lot* carried away."

"Me, too."

"I don't want to rush you."

"We're moving too fast." Pressing her hot face against his shirt, Brandy heard his heart beating rapidly beneath her cheek. Felt the swift rise and fall of his chest. He'd been as swept away as she. If she hadn't come to her senses in time, they would have . . . Well, they definitely would have. Five years of good intentions — annihilated. What a scary discovery she'd made about herself.

"Right." He took a deep breath and leaned his head back on the sofa cushion.

"We have to be careful."

"I wear asbestos gloves when I play with fire," he said with a wry grin. "Is that the kind of careful you mean?"

"Whatever will keep us from getting burned." She couldn't give in to the desire he'd ignited. It was too soon. No matter how tempting Trick was, no matter how cherished and alive his kisses made her feel, she could not — would not — have a casual affair with her boss. She had to think of her future. Of Chloe's future.

Getting involved with a man so clearly *not* into commitment was heartbreak waiting to happen. Thirty-seven-year-old bachelors got that way for a reason. Unlike her, they weren't interested in marriage. No doubt, Trick preferred flings with willing women. She wasn't willing, and flings weren't her style.

"I respect you, Brandy." Trick pulled back, putting a little physical distance between them. "I won't take advantage of you or the situation."

"I appreciate that. I know all about situations," she said grimly. "Maybe I should tell you why I married Joe."

"I'd like to know everything about you." She was tied up in knots, but Trick was relaxed and attentive. A master of self-restraint. Hard to believe a man could tamp down the heat that had sparked between them a few short moments ago. But then, he was an expert who controlled fire for a living.

"I was nineteen when I met Joe. He was

the first man I ever . . . well, let's just say, I was naive." Heat rose in her cheeks. At least she hadn't switched on lights when they returned from the park. She wasn't accustomed to talking about private matters and the late-afternoon shadows hid her embarrassment. "Slapdown is a very small town and can only support one bad boy. For years, Joe was it. Handsome. Dangerous. Exciting. You know the drill."

Trick nodded. "He was the town's wild card, and you were the good girl who thought she could 'tame' him."

She laughed, but not with amusement. A sharp note of sarcasm cut her tone. "Common sense, and everyone who knew me tried to convince me otherwise. I wouldn't listen. I was in love. Deep down, I knew Joe was bad for me, but I just knew I could change him. He was misunderstood and hurting. All he needed for redemption was the healing power of my love."

"And?"

"I couldn't save him from his own self-destructive nature, but I did get a surprise." When one of his dark brows lifted in question, she continued. "I became pregnant with Chloe."

"I see." Trick didn't judge. For that she was grateful. He let her tell the story in her own way. In her own time.

"We did the right thing. We got married, but we never really worked as a couple. The only thing we had going for us was physical attraction. Maybe some unfulfilled needs neither of us understood. When the attraction faded, we could no longer satisfy each other's needs. We woke up one day and realized we didn't have much in common."

"A bad experience." Trick's sympathy sounded sincere, and Brandy was glad she'd had the courage to talk about the past. Acknowledging mistakes made her less likely to repeat them.

"I prefer to call it a 'learning' experience," she said with a wry grin.

"Do you think *we* have anything in common?" he asked.

"One thing, for sure."

"What's that?"

"We're both lonelier than we should be."

"You're right about that." He leaned closer, as though pulled back into the magnetic force of their attraction against his will. He was going to kiss her again, and if he did, she might not be able to stop this time.

"I'm thirsty. How about you? Want a soft drink?" Brandy jumped to her feet. Trick was doing and saying everything right. Like he understood what she was thinking, feeling. Nothing made a man more appealing than empathy. If she didn't keep her hands busy in a constructive way, she might forget her good intentions.

"Sure." He followed her into the kitchen and leaned against the counter. "I think we have more in common than loneliness and just haven't discovered what it is yet."

She handed him a can of cola from the fridge, then a glass filled with ice. "Maybe. But we'll never know if we jump right into . . ."

"Sex?" he supplied.

And that's all it could be at the moment. She wanted more. She wanted the soul-deep bond that making love to the right man would forge. "Sex complicates everything. It creates a different kind of connection. Physical, not emotional. There's only one way to find out if there's more sparking between us than chemistry."

"And that is?"

"We have to take things slowly. Get better acquainted. See what develops."

He groaned, pulled the ring tab and poured the beverage over the ice. Took a long sip. "Was it in the CIA where you learned torture tactics?"

She smiled. "If you're only interested in sex, I'm sure you can find that elsewhere."

He nearly choked on his drink. "Are you always so honest?"

"I try to be. I don't like to play games."

"Me, either. I admire a straight-talking woman."

"Good." She leaned on the opposite counter and sipped her own drink. "Here's some more straight talk. I need to make something clear up-front. I won't have a casual affair with you. I need more than that."

He nodded. "I know. I've always known what you need."

"And you're still . . . interested?"

"Well, yeah." He frowned, his dark brows drawing together. "Did you expect me to bolt for the door at the first mention of commitment?"

"Frankly, yes." She laughed. "Isn't that how you've managed to remain unattached for so long?"

"Maybe." Trick smiled. He wasn't nearly as honest as Brandy and knew enough to hedge his bets. Bluffing was a hard habit to break. He couldn't show his cards. Not yet.

She tipped her glass of cola with the same resolve another person might chug down hard liquor. "I've done my bit for the

Bad Boy Redemption Program. I've learned my lesson."

She flushed, rosy color rising in her cheeks. Trick wanted, needed, to kiss her again. No. What he needed was to cool off. If he didn't, he might lose the control he'd struggled to maintain. "Let's go sit on the porch." Outside, in full view of the neighborhood, he'd have to keep his hands to himself.

Brandy peeked in on a sleeping Chloe before following him out. They sat side by side on the creaky wooden swing, and he set it into gentle motion. "It's nice out here," he said.

"I like to come out after Chloe's down for the night. Helps me unwind."

Did he ever unwind? At the end of a hard day, he collapsed into bed, slept without dreams and awoke the next morning to start all over again. He recharged his batteries by taking on more work. By never slowing long enough to take stock of his life. Since meeting Brandy, he was constantly measuring his past against the future. His sleep was restless, his dreams vivid.

They sat in companionable silence as dusk tucked in the quiet neighborhood for the night. All along the block, lights flickered on, casting a warm glow through open windows. Down the street, children laughed and called to one another, raced home on bicycles. Dinners simmered inside houses, and mingled aromas lingered on the still air. Roasting meat and cinnamon?

He was an interloper here, but Brandy's home sheltered him in a way his mostly empty, uninviting apartment never had. Never would. He felt safe here. Maybe because the slower pace recalled time he'd spent in his grandmother's house, snugged into a hollow of the Ozark Mountains. On summer evenings, they'd sat on the veranda after supper, watching fireflies flicker among the trees. Granny Bett had told him he'd never be lost because the lightning bugs would show him the way home.

But he did feel lost. He no longer had a home. Brandy was right. He *had* been running all his life. As a kid, he'd run to catch up with parents who never had time for him. As a young man, he'd run to stay ahead of the pack. He'd kept the company afloat after his father's death by not having a life of his own.

So what was his excuse now? When it came to relationships, he ran at the first sign of involvement. He hadn't lost his heart to a woman because he'd convinced himself he didn't have a heart to lose. Maybe he'd been wrong. Maybe he just hadn't met the right woman. For the first time, he was not only willing to risk losing his heart; he was willing to *give* it away.

To Brandy.

"You're awfully quiet," she said after a few minutes.

"I was thinking about what you said earlier," he said softly. "About running. You know, that gets old after a while. Especially when you've forgotten why you entered the race in the first place." He turned to face her. "I never wanted a home and family."

She tensed beside him, and her lips pulled into a tight smile. "I figured as much."

"Until now," he hastened to add. "You make me want things I never thought I could have."

"I guess we're even," she murmured softly. "You make me feel things I never thought I could feel."

It took all his self-control not to pull her into his arms and cover her sweet face with kisses. He wanted this woman, but was *he* right for *her?* What if he didn't deserve her? What if he wasn't good enough? He'd never considered such issues before. Maybe because he'd never trusted anyone enough to open himself up to the possibilities. He didn't know if he could start now.

Even old war dogs can learn new tricks with the right motivation. And the right reward.

With Brandy's help, he might learn how to love. Learn how to be the kind of man she needed. He had to be careful. There was too much at stake to rush in and spoil things. Not just for him, but for Brandy. And Chloe. He couldn't blow what might be his only chance for real happiness.

"So where do we go from here?" she asked.

"We have to give ourselves time."

She sighed. With relief? Frustration? "What do you have in mind?"

She was good at asking hard questions, but he didn't have easy answers. He didn't know what to do.

"Maybe we should start by going out on a real date," he suggested. "Would you have dinner with me tomorrow night?"

She didn't hesitate. "I might have trouble finding a sitter on Sunday. Can I call you tomorrow and let you know?"

"If you can't find anyone, we'll take Chloe with us." Now that he'd made up his mind, he couldn't take no for an answer.

"It wouldn't be a real date then, would it?" She gave him a shy smile.

"No, it wouldn't." He had to kiss her again. So he did. In front of anyone who cared to look.

"Where are you going again, Mommy?" Chloe bounced onto Brandy's bed. She stretched out on her stomach with her chin in her palms and watched her mother pull dresses from the closet.

"Just out to eat." Brandy rejected her best black dress. Too serious. She was nervous, but also hopeful. Maybe she'd finally found the right thing. She was wary, too. She couldn't afford to be burned again. What if her feelings for Trick were just physical attraction disguised as the real thing? Had dating always been so complicated?

She laughed. How would she know? She wasn't exactly an Olympic-level dater. She continued to sift through the closet's contents until she spotted her favorite gray skirt. That was more like it. If she paired the skirt with a blue sweater set, she would be well dressed without looking like she was trying too hard. She didn't want Trick to think she was coming on too strong.

"Out to eat with Trick?" Chloe asked.

"Uh-huh."

"Are you going to Mister Cheesie's again?"

Brandy zipped the straight skirt and ruffled her daughter's hair. "No. I'm pretty sure we won't be going to Mister Cheesie's tonight." She hoped Trick wouldn't take her to a fancy, expensive restaurant. They were going on a date, but candlelight and white tablecloths and flowers would put too much pressure on what she hoped would be a simple "getting to know you" evening. Unnecessarily romantic elements would just make it harder to resist the lure of mutual attraction.

Someone knocked on the door, and Chloe jumped off the bed. "I'll get it."

"That's probably Amy." Fortunately for Brandy, college students always needed extra money. Chloe's after-school caregiver had seemed happy to baby-sit on such short notice.

The seafood restaurant Trick selected was perfect. The atmosphere was more fun than fancy, and the ambient noise level encouraged conversation without making it difficult. They talked about current events and local news over crab cake appetizers. They discussed Hotspur while enjoying broiled salmon steaks, and Brandy learned how the business had taken the place of family in Trick's life. By the time coffee and dessert were served, they had tackled more personal topics. Brandy was surprised at how easy it was to talk to Trick. Busy and distracted at work, tonight he gave her his full attention.

When he turned all that high-beam intensity on her, Trick's full attention was impossible to resist. He was big on eye contact, and at times, she felt like she was drowning in the depths of his gaze. If he could make her all hot and bothered over dinner, what would it be like to have his intense concentration in the bedroom? The term spontaneous combustion came to mind. She gulped ice water to douse those flaming mental images.

They shared details of their childhoods and made interesting discoveries. Both were only children who'd grown up without siblings. Both had learned at an early age not to depend on their parents, for different reasons.

"We never stayed in one place for long." The frequent moves had been a source of anxiety to Brandy. She'd always been an outsider, afraid of making friends for fear of losing them. "Mom often said Dad had 'a rambling spirit.' I guess that made him sound less irresponsible and more adventurous."

"At least they didn't leave you behind when they took off," Trick pointed out. "My mother followed my father around the country while he chased after fires, and I ended up staying with my grandmother. I always felt a little unnecessary to them."

Maybe that was another reason he focused all his energy on his job. He was very protective of his men and had spent years building his business. He had no family ties. Working long, hard hours was the only way he could feel necessary. As much as she wanted to tell him how important he could be to her, to Chloe, Brandy bit back her words. He wasn't ready to hear them. She'd bide her time. Show him, without words, what he could mean to them.

"My problem was the opposite. My parents depended on me too much. My mother was sick a lot, and my father was terrible with the details of daily living. I had to take on the caretaking role as I got older."

He smiled. "That explains why you're so independent."

"I don't know about that, but it probably explains why I'm so good at juggling priorities."

"Do your parents still depend on you?"

"Not as much. They finally settled down when I was in high school, because I refused to be uprooted again. Dad found a decent job, which he's managed to keep. Mom had back surgery a couple of years ago, and he really came through for her. I think he realized how lost he'd be without her. It's been a relief not to be so responsible for their happiness."

"And yet you chose a marriage like the one your parents had."

She thought about that. "I guess you're right. Joe was irresponsible and undependable. I just continued in the role I'd grown up in."

"It's time someone took care of you."

She laughed. "I won't hold my breath." The conversation had reactivated her worries. Trick's footloose bachelor ways might make it impossible for him to settle down. To accept the responsibility of family life. Was she just jumping out of a cooling frying pan into the fire?

The waiter refilled their coffee cups, giving them an excuse to linger a little longer. Brandy was glad to stay. The more she learned about Trick, the more she liked him. Maybe they weren't all about physical attraction. She tried to find other interests in common, but it soon became apparent that he didn't take time to read books or go to movies. He rarely watched anything except news on TV. She teased him about being pop culturally deprived and promised to introduce him to some of her interests. Teaching him to have fun could be one of the most enjoyable things she'd ever done.

Trick walked Brandy to her door an hour later. "I had a great time tonight."

"Me, too." Things had gone well. Maybe too well. Was she headed for another heartbreak? One date, and she was hooked. If Trick never asked her out again, she would be crushed. She'd already invested so much in their tenuous future.

"Are you going to feel uncomfortable at the office tomorrow?" he asked. "After all, you're dating the boss now."

She soaked up his comment the way a thirsty rose soaked up Miracle Gro. Dating the boss. Maybe he *did* feel as invested as she did. "I don't think so." She would be honest. "We're going about this the right way. If we don't let the physical side of things get out of control, we'll be fine."

He clasped her upper arms and pulled her close. "Would a good-night kiss be considered out of control?"

"No." She tipped her lips up to his. She'd been anticipating this moment all day. Trick had vowed to respect the boundaries, but it was up to her to set them. And she would. Confident, at least for the moment, she smiled. "A good-night kiss, after a lovely evening, seems highly appropriate to me."

Chapter Ten

Tired of fighting the internal voice steering him in Brandy's direction, Trick decided to pay attention. Warily. He'd been doing things his way for years. Following his head. Ignoring his feelings. Shutting people out. Maybe it was time to try a new approach. However, surrendering his longtime bachelor status was just as hard as he thought it would be.

Once he stopped resisting what his heart tried to tell him, he had no idea what to do next. He was a total stranger to courtship and had never stumbled anywhere remotely near the vicinity of true love. He couldn't woo Brandy the way he tackled other important projects. With born-again zeal and goal-oriented enthusiasm. He had no one to turn to for advice, so he was forced to listen to his subconscious.

Be patient. No nut is harder to crack than a bachelor cynic.

Learning to accept unsolicited bits of wisdom from his subconscious, Trick could no longer deny his feelings for

Brandy. Feelings were the problem. The concept of fateful true love shook him to the core. How was he supposed to trust something he'd always considered as real as unicorns and elves? The possibility that he might have a chance for happily-ever-after with Brandy was more frightening than the hottest fire he'd ever faced.

When he was with Brandy, he felt good about their relationship and the progress he was making. However, when they were apart, the old doubts crept back. He was too much of a realist to believe he could just settle down after a lifetime of freedom. What if he couldn't give Brandy the security she needed? It was hard to think outside the Hotspur box he'd been living in for fifteen years.

Thankfully, the restrictions Brandy placed on their relationship kept things from becoming overheated and complicated. Which taught him another lesson. Sex without love was very different from being in love without having sex. A novice at emotional involvement, Trick had never considered his past encounters meaning-less. They just hadn't been relevant in the big picture. He'd unerringly chosen women who didn't object to him keeping his heart out of the equation. As a result, sex without love had never been a problem.

Love without physical release was a bit dicier. Brandy's hands-off-for-now rule fueled his desire and at the same time, forced him to face his feelings. Taken out of the context of sexual gratification, his emotions seemed more reliable. Not that he didn't want the physical part. He did. On a constant, aching basis.

However, he was convinced he was finally doing something right for all the right reasons. He would make do with passionate kisses. For now. He respected their agreed-upon limits and took a lot of cold showers.

See? Love is all it's cracked up to be.

Love. He still had trouble using the term, but something *was* different. Now when he was working in the field, he found excuses to stop by the office. Seeing Brandy confirmed his longing and made it real. He found truth in the dark warm depths of her gaze. Not only was he capable of being crazy about her, it was possible she felt the same way about him.

When he couldn't get to the office, he called in. He couldn't make it through the day without hearing her voice at least five times. He'd never required that much contact with anyone before. He had to spend every free moment with her, because when they were apart, he wasn't living, he was waiting. Waiting to get back to her. Waiting to talk to her. Waiting to touch her and lose all doubts in her kiss.

The warm days of Indian summer shortened into autumn, and despite his former objections, Trick slipped into the comforting routine of domestic life. Brandy's quiet strength helped him batter down the emotional barriers he'd hidden behind for so long. She and Chloe tapped into a tenderness he hadn't known he possessed. He was a better man with them than he was without them.

All the more reason to worry.

He'd never needed anyone before, but he needed Brandy. It still wasn't clear if she needed him, but whenever he questioned his worthiness, that infernal internal cheerleader leapt up to allay his fears. Sometimes the encouraging messages were practical.

Look how far you've come in such a short time.

Don't be so hard on yourself; you're making progress.

Other times they promoted a less existential philosophy.

Finding the person born to complete you is the reason you exist.

Loving Brandy fulfills your life's purpose.

Such uncharacteristic thoughts troubled him at first, but they were so persistent, he had to come to terms with the urging of his subconscious. Unless he believed he could have it all, he never would. Love. Security. Home and family. Happiness. He had to trust that his heart knew what his mind resisted. That Brandy would stick with him to the end. She would be there to hold his hand when he died. He could live on in the memories of the children and grandchildren she would give him.

Deep and unsettling for a guy who had always lived in the moment.

Another thing Trick learned was how to have fun for fun's sake. He discovered he enjoyed playing with Chloe, walking with her and Brandy to the park to feed the ducks. He raked autumn leaves into piles and laughed when Chloe tossed them by the handfuls. On weekends, they made popcorn and watched movies. Brandy and Chloe introduced him to their favorite films, which became his favorites too. They made hot chocolate on cool evenings, lemonade on warm afternoons. Trick helped Chloe make snickerdoodles, and the baking cookies filled the kitchen with the sweet scent of sugar and cinnamon.

Letting others into his life was a big, dangerous step for a loner to take, but definitely worth the risk.

One breezy Sunday afternoon in late October, Trick climbed a stepladder to scoop leaves from Brandy's gutters. His thoughts flashed back to the day they'd met. He'd harshly condemned what he now cherished most. A few weeks ago, he'd been afraid to fall into Brandy Mitchum's domestic snare. Now he worried she might examine her catch more closely and not deem him a keeper. He'd had a taste of happiness. A glimpse of what his life could be. Like Chloe, he still had trouble distinguishing between what was real and what he only wanted to be real, but it was difficult to imagine a future without Brandy and her little girl.

A car horn honked, and he looked down as Joe Mitchum's shiny black SUV pulled into the driveway. Chloe was home from spending the weekend with her father.

"Hey, Trick! Look what I got!" Chloe jumped out, and her father's little white dog bounced after her, following her around to the back of the car. She reappeared, her little arms wrapped around a huge pumpkin. Joe bore most of the weight. His wife Mallory set Chloe's overnight bag on the porch, and the dog leaped in a happy circle.

"That's a whopper of a pumpkin, Little Bit." Trick climbed down the ladder to join the group. Joe grinned, set the pumpkin on the sidewalk and walked back to the car.

"I got four more. Can you believe it?" Chloe's breathlessness wasn't due to exertion. It came from finding magic in something as simple as a big orange gourd. Viewed through a child's eyes, old experiences were new. Common events were miracles. Trick now appreciated things he'd never noticed before. The artistry of a pretty red leaf flattened on the sidewalk after a rain. The marvel of a wooly caterpillar inching along a dry stalk. The brilliance of the evening's first star. Chloe had opened his eyes.

"You do?"

"Yep. One for every year old I am. Where's Mommy? I want to show her."

"She ran to the store. She'll be back in a minute," Trick said.

"We stopped by the pumpkin patch at the church charity lot on the way," Joe explained as he deposited the other pumpkins in a festive row. "We went a little wild. I hope Brandy won't mind."

"She mentioned she wanted to decorate the yard for fall. These will be a good start." Though their divorce had been painful at the time, Trick knew Brandy and Joe maintained amicable terms for Chloe's sake. Her ability to leave the past behind, to let go of pain and learn from it, was a quality he admired.

Trick thumped the star of the pumpkin show. "This big guy's gonna make a great jack-o'-lantern."

"Will you carve it, Trick?" Chloe asked. "A funny face, not a scary one."

Trick hesitated. Joe was Chloe's father. He had first claim on jack-o'-lantern duties. Trick was . . . well, what he was to Chloe had yet to be defined.

Joe spoke up. "If Trick's not too busy, I'm sure he'll have time to carve the pumpkin. Mommy can help you paint faces on the little ones."

"Sure." Oddly enough, Trick was never too busy these days. It was a liberating feeling. He gave Joe a quick nod, universal guy code for "thanks, pal." Joe nodded back as Mallory linked her arm in his. The dog raced around the yard.

He'd met Brandy's ex-husband a couple of times before. He'd been prepared to dislike the man who'd broken her heart but felt no animosity toward him. Joe had been lost for years, but he was honorable and kind. Brandy had been unable to save him, but another woman had. He'd overcome enormous problems and was a good father to Chloe. A loving husband to the second wife who'd helped him turn his life around. Joe and Mallory Mitchum were a solid example of the healing power of love.

After Joe and Mallory left, Trick sat on the porch step with Chloe to wait for Brandy. "What are you going to do with all those pumpkins?"

"I have to take one to school for the fall festival. Will you come?"

"What's the fall festival?"

"It's a carnival. There's popcorn and candy and cakewalks. We buy tickets and play games in the gym and win prizes."

"Sounds like fun." Surprisingly, it did.

"I have to wear a costume, but you don't unless you want to." Chloe leaned close. "Please say you'll come. Please, please."

"When is this extravaganza?"

"I'm not too good with calendars yet." Chloe considered. "But it's the day before Halloween and starts at six o'clock. Promise you'll come."

So this was what it felt like to be included. A new and heartwarming sensation. "Sure. I wouldn't miss it."

"Goody!" She clapped her hands and changed the subject. "Celestian dug a hole in Mallory's flower bed, and I filled it back up."

"You're a good helper. What about the other Celestian?"

"The one who's not a dog? I made him stay here with you and Mommy."

"I guess you don't really need him anymore." Trick and Brandy had discussed Chloe's imaginary friend and decided not to let the issue turn into a power struggle. He'd told Brandy about his own playmate and how Billy the Dragon had left on his own when he was no longer needed. Lately Chloe hadn't mentioned the pretend Celestian much. She seemed happy and settled in school with new friends. Trick liked to think his presence in Chloe's life made an invisible playmate less necessary.

She propped her elbows on her knees and rested her chin in her palms. "Celestian is really here to help you and Mommy, not me. I don't need help. I'm pretty smart for my age."

"Yes, you are. But Mommy and I are grown-ups. We don't need Celestian's help, either."

"Uh-huh. You do. You wouldn't be

Mommy's boyfriend without him."

"Is that so?" Her words made him smile. Mommy's boyfriend. He could live with that for now. Maybe someday he would be more. Mommy's husband. Chloe's step-daddy.

She sighed. "I'm not supposed to —" she paused "— reveal privileged information. Miss Steuban says you can eat the seeds inside pumpkins."

"If you roast them, you can." Trick smiled at how deftly Chloe changed the subject. Her nimble mind flitted like a butterfly from one topic to another.

"I don't want to roast my pumpkin's seeds. I want to put them in the ground and grow some for next year. We planted beans in class, in paper cups. They turned into bean plants."

"That's how it works. Planting the seeds is a good idea."

"Our part is easy." Chloe looked up and smiled. "Tuck 'em into bed and let Mother Nature work her magic."

"Right." Trick gave the child a quick hug. Funny. Granny Bett used to say the same thing when she planted her spring garden. Chloe's words carried him back to a cool Ozark morning, over thirty years ago. He'd been no older than Chloe when his grandmother showed him how to drop tiny seeds into the freshly turned earth and rake a soil "coverlet" over them with his hand. "Where'd you hear about Mother Nature?" he asked.

Brandy arrived, and Chloe jumped up to greet her. She stopped, looked over her shoulder and said, "Everyone knows about Mother Nature, silly."

A week later, Brandy was working at the computer when attorney Charles Thorson stopped by the office. "Sorry, Charles. You just missed Trick. He has a meeting in Lubbock and won't be back until later tonight."

Charles settled in the chair across from Brandy's desk. "That's all right. I'm not here to see Trick. I came to talk to you."

"What can I do for you?" She saved the letter she was working on and turned away from the monitor.

"In all the times we've talked, you never mentioned you're a paralegal."

"No big secret." She shrugged. "I guess the subject never came up."

"Mind if I ask where you received your training?"

"The business school in Midland. Why do you ask?"

"Trick was in the office the other day so I could prep him for his deposition, and he mentioned you've been volunteering downtown at Legal Aid."

"Yes, for a few weeks now. Mostly on Saturdays when my daughter visits her father. Researching precedents and helping prepare legal documents keeps my skills sharp, and I enjoy helping people."

"Getting certified isn't easy. Don't you want to work in the profession you trained for?"

"Sure. But there aren't many available paralegal jobs in Odessa."

"Trick mentioned you're working at Hotspur until you find another job."

"He did?" Charles nodded, and her stomach tightened. Trick had been much more open lately, but he always expected people to leave. That's why he was so reluctant to let anyone get close. "That was our agreement when I started. However, I haven't been looking. I enjoy working at Hotspur."

"You're loyal. I like that." Charles smiled. "What if a job found you? Would you consider changing employment?"

"I don't know. What do you have in mind?"

"Are you familiar with the Indigent Defense Fund?"

"Sure." She smiled. "Everyone is entitled to legal representation, and if a defendant can't afford an attorney, one will be appointed."

"Right. I've been contacted by the criminal court system to take on some cases. It's not pro bono. There's a nominal fee involved. As much as I believe in justice for all, I can't commit to more work unless I have help."

Brandy knew the law practice had been a one-man operation since Charles' father retired. The only employee was a legal secretary. "Why me?"

"Funny you should ask. When Trick mentioned you were a paralegal, I didn't think much about it. After he left, I opened the mail and there was the indigent defense offer. Knowing I couldn't take on extra work, I figured I'd have to turn it down. Then I got a strange yearning for a scone. Normally I don't even like scones."

Brandy frowned. "A scone made you think of me?"

"Yeah. I went across the street to the coffee shop and bought one to go. I bit into it on the way back to the office, and your name popped into my head."

"It wasn't a cinnamon scone was it?"

Charles grinned. "How'd you know?"

"Just a lucky guess." The taste or scent of cinnamon had given her lots of strange ideas in the past months. Never underestimate the hallucinogenic properties of common spices.

"I'm willing to pay a good paralegal excellent wages to perform the same duties you're doing at Legal Aid for free."

"I don't want to give up working at Legal Aid," she told Charles. "It's been very rewarding."

"You wouldn't have to quit volunteering. What you do on your own time is your business. I know you have a child and need your evenings free. Trick told me. I can guarantee you forty hours a week. If my practice expands, I can use help in areas other than indigent defense. I'm willing to match your current salary and benefits. Maybe even top it. Are you interested?"

Of course, she was interested. She dreamed of working for the defense of others. To speak for those without voices. Championing the underdog was the reason she'd become a paralegal. Her brief stint at Futterman-Ulbright had been less than fulfilling because the clients didn't always deserve the settlements they received.

Brandy folded her arms on her desk. "There's something I should tell you. I was

241

fired from my last paralegal job."

"I know all about that." Charles shrugged. "If Fenton Futterman didn't like you, I *know* you're good. Being fired by that slimy weasel is all the recommendation I need."

"Really?"

"I wouldn't be here if I had doubts about your ability to handle the job."

"Does Trick know about this?"

Charles shook his head. "I'm a lawyer, not a saint. I wanted to talk to you first."

"I'm tempted, but I can't bail out on Trick. He depends on me to keep things running smoothly here."

"I know. He sings your praises all the time."

"He does?"

"Constantly. Despite what he may have told you about me, you'll find I'm easy to get along with. I need someone who can work independently, without constant supervision. Once we start taking on defense cases, you'll have plenty of opportunity to make a significant contribution. I think you'll find the work rewarding."

"Yes, I'm sure I would. However, Trick hired me when no one else would. I can't leave him in a bind."

"I understand. Trick's my friend. I don't stab friends in the back. Find someone to take your place. Spend as much time as you need to train your replacement. I don't want any hard feelings if you decide to accept my offer." Charles grinned and added in a conspiratorial tone, "I'm on retainer to Hotspur. As much as I'd hate to lose Trick as a friend, I'd hate to lose him as a client even more."

"It's a generous offer. Can I think about it?"

"I have until the end of November to accept or reject the IDF contract. Is that enough time?"

"Yes. I want to talk to Trick and make sure he's okay with me leaving. I need to find a new office manager." As much as Brandy would like to return to the legal profession, she had to weigh her options.

Trick had hired her when she was desperate and without prospects. Still, he'd reminded her in the past that if a better job came along, she was free to take it. Instead of reassuring her, his open-door policy had threatened the security she craved. Made her work harder to become indispensable. Which she liked to think she was now. Would he understand? Or would he consider her leaving another form of abandonment?

Things had been going well between them the past three weeks. As hard as it had been not to be swept away, they'd respected their agreement, confining physical contact to kisses and caresses. If she weren't his employee, and he weren't her boss, perhaps they could take their relationship to the next level.

Charles stood. "I understand. I wouldn't want it any other way." He removed a business card from his wallet and placed it on her desk. "Call me when you reach a decision."

"I'd appreciate it if you didn't mention this to Trick until I've had a chance to talk to him."

"Of course. I look forward to hearing from you."

After Charles left, Brandy called Mr. Johnson at Flash Personnel about a replacement. She wouldn't mention Charles' offer to Trick without having a contingency plan.

The unemployment situation hadn't improved much in the weeks she'd been at Hotspur. The employment counselor told her he would look over his files and let her know. He warned that it might take some time to find a qualified applicant and suggested she run a newspaper ad.

She thanked him and asked him to let her know if he found someone. She hung up the phone, more discouraged than she'd been in weeks. Why would such a wonderful opportunity arise, if she couldn't take it?

Maybe this was a test. *Was* she loyal? Could she put her own wants and needs aside for a man she'd come to care about? Would she have to? They'd grown closer, but she still wasn't sure where their relationship was headed. He'd demonstrated an ability to focus on something other than work, but his job hadn't been very demanding lately. What would happen when things picked up, and he had to head off to fire sites for days, even weeks, at a time?

She didn't begrudge the attention he lavished on his work. His occupation was an essential part of who he was. But her work was important, too. She thought of Charles' offer and sighed. There had to be an answer to this dilemma. She went to the back to get a diet cola out of the refrigerator and changed her mind. Cola wasn't what she wanted.

Maybe she'd have a nice hot cup of cinnamon tea instead.

H.A.R.P. Emergency Communiqué
From: Mission Control
To: Celestian, Earthbound Operative
Mission: Operation True Love
Subject: Cease and Desist Order

ALERT! It has come to our attention that results documented in previous Field Reports may be negatively skewed due to operative's unauthorized use of thought manipulation and dream tampering. Trifling with a subject's free will is not a deployable strategy.

Repeat: Interfering with free will is forbidden! Manipulation of ideas other than subject's own is strictly prohibited, and restrictions are clearly outlined in Section Five of the current policy and procedures manual, a copy of which was provided prior to initiation of mission.

Operative is authorized to use *only* environmental controls and management of events to complete mission. Further use of unsanctioned techniques will not be tolerated. Failure to adhere to policy will result in immediate termination of mission, summary recall of operative and withdrawal of all reward offers.

If acknowledgement of this transmission is not received by Central Command within twenty-four hours, immediate termination procedures will be initiated.

H.A.R.P. Field Report
From: Celestian, Earthbound Operative
To: Mission Control
Subject: Operation True Love

Progress Report: Emergency communiqué received and hereby acknowledged. Failure to abide by guidelines due in part to operative's mistaken assumption that all *is* fair in love and war. Have reviewed Section Five of PPM and will establish new goals based on acceptable use of limited resources. Current objectives were met, but successful outcome of mission can no longer be assured.

Plan: Unknown at this time.

Chapter Eleven

Overnight, the lengthy dry spell at Hotspur ended, and Trick was suddenly swamped with work. He met the challenge with his usual enthusiasm, joking that someone must have left the gate to hell open. Brandy regretted the sudden increase in business after the lull that had allowed them to spend so much time together, but the effect on Trick was obvious. He was relieved and eager to get back into harness.

She'd been so happy the past few weeks. She'd assumed he was content to spend quiet time with her and Chloe. Clearly, he thrived on pressure and missed being at the epicenter of Hurricane Hotspur. Baking cookies and watching kiddie videos could hardly compete with the kind of drama he was used to. He relished the opportunity to refocus his attention on putting out fires. The literal instead of the figurative variety they'd both been trying to control the past weeks. It was crazy to think a man who'd spent half his life solving one crisis after another would be content to rake leaves and carve pumpkins for long.

She didn't get a chance to talk to him about Charles' job offer. The representative of an offshore drilling company called to invite him to inspect their Mississippi Gulf operation and place a bid for well-control services. He jumped at the chance, and the trip took him away for a couple of days. Later, he was asked to fill in for a scheduled speaker at a regional petroleum industry conference and was gone most of the weekend. By the time he returned, an unusual number of consultation requests had piled up. Then there were the call-outs that kept him and the crew hopping from one fire site to another.

Trick never missed a beat. He jumped back into overtime mode, tackling the onslaught as though the time he'd spent with her had never happened.

Now, Brandy rarely spoke to Trick more than once a day. A rushed accounting of where he was off to next. He hadn't had dinner with her and Chloe for two weeks. He worked so late, he rarely had time to stop by even for a quick visit. He checked in at the office on the fly, grabbing messages and noting the appointments she made for him. Even his kisses were distracted and perfunctory. As though his mind was already miles ahead of his body.

Brandy's own body ached to hold him. She'd been aching a lot lately. Even the dreams had started up again. Trick's absence had opened the door of her subconscious, and the Midnight Man had slipped back in. The only thing was, he was no longer a stranger. She knew him all too well. Why had she never realized before that the man in her dreams was Trick?

Had always been Trick.

Late one evening, just before dark, she stepped out the front door with the broom, intent on clearing drifted autumn leaves from the porch. If she stayed busy, she wouldn't notice how much she missed Trick. How much she'd come to depend on him. Depending on him was a mistake. So was relying on dream men. She had to get back in touch with the real world.

She swept fiercely, clearing the porch, but was unable to clear the clutter of thoughts from her mind. The quiet moments and simple fun they'd shared had been little more than a brief intermission in the road show of Trick Templeton's life. A momentary diversion before he returned to his real world.

She'd known all along he was married to

his job. Like an infant who hid her face and thought no one could see her, she'd deluded herself into thinking if she didn't acknowledge the truth, it wouldn't be true. Unfortunately reality was not the imagined, idealized version of the future she wanted with Trick.

Somehow, during the past few weeks, she'd lost sight of the basic differences between them. She'd trusted her feelings, when common sense was much more reliable. Trick's attention and tenderness had given her a false sense of security. She'd believed, for a while, that she might be enough for him. She'd been swept away by the first man to ignite a smoldering spark of desire in a heart grown cold. Let her wants take precedent over her needs by loving a man who wasn't cut out for the long haul. Would she ever learn not to let emotion dictate action?

No matter how attractive Trick was, no matter how cherished and special he made her feel, one indisputable fact remained. He wasn't what she needed. With the porch cleared, Brandy sat on the swing. He'd seemed at home in her little house. He'd taken out the trash and stood at the counter chopping onions. He'd read Chloe stories. He claimed he enjoyed peace and calm, but his heart was always hovering on the horizon, waiting for the next adventure. He probably didn't even realize that what he *said* he wanted would never be enough. Forcing him into a role for which he was temperamentally unsuited was a recipe for disaster.

She'd made this same mistake with Joe. She'd unintentionally trapped him with her pregnancy. She'd expected him to take on responsibilities he couldn't handle. She'd tried to wish him into changing. Expected him to be something he couldn't be. He'd sunk deeper and deeper into depression, and it had taken a bolt of lightning and the right woman to open his eyes.

She'd mistakenly believed that moving to Odessa and working for Fenton Futterman would give her the fresh start she couldn't have at home. She'd imagined the sacrifices had been worth it. Fantasized that Futterman would someday realize what a hard worker she was and reward her efforts. She'd been fired instead.

Brandy went inside. No wonder Chloe preferred make-believe to reality.

She picked up scattered books and toys and carried them to her daughter's room. Chloe spent way too much time alone these days. She stopped in the hall and listened. Chloe was singing an old rhyme Trick had learned from his grandmother. One flew east. One flew west. One flew over the cuckoo's nest. She should have realized how much her little girl missed Trick.

For a while, Chloe had seemed willing to let go of Celestian, but her invisible friend had taken on new importance in Trick's absence. She insisted on taking Celestian to school again despite the conflict he caused. Brandy hated watching her normally cheerful child drag her feet instead of running happily into the classroom.

Inside her room, Chloe stopped singing and raised her voice in frustration. These days, poor make-believe Celestian took the brunt of her disappointment. She projected the anger she couldn't express to Trick on the hapless figment of her imagination.

"Well, you're not doing a very good job!" she snapped in a very un-Chloe-like fit of temper. "You're a crummy guide."

"I think you did something wrong. That's why Trick went away. It's your fault, and I'm mad at you. You got me in trouble today. You're not my friend anymore!"

Brandy knocked. Chloe invited her in, and she sat on the bed and pulled her pajama-clad daughter onto her lap. Fresh from her bath, she had that "clean kid" smell every mother loved. Mingled with the bubble gum scented bubble bath she used was the smell of cinnamon. She'd had a cinnamon toast snack earlier, and Brandy checked her pajamas for crumbs.

She tried using an "I" message as suggested by a parenting magazine article she'd read. "Honey, I get worried when I see you so upset."

"I'm sorry, Mommy."

"Why don't you tell me what's bothering you."

"It's Celestian."

"What did he do?"

"He messed up. He got me in trouble at school today."

"How?"

"It was on the playground. Spencer teased me. I tried to run away, but he followed me. He said Celestian wasn't real and when I said uh-huh, yes, he is, Spencer called me a big fat liar. He said my pants were on fire."

Brandy smoothed Chloe's hair back from her forehead. "That must have hurt your feelings."

"No. It made me mad! I shoved Spencer and he fell down and started crying. The big baby!"

"What happened then?"

"Miss Steuban came and made me apologize."

"Did that make you feel better?"

"No. Spencer didn't deserve an I'm sorry."

"If you hurt him, you had to tell him you were sorry."

"Even if I wasn't?" Chloe looked up, her small face troubled. "Even if he was being a poo-poo head?"

"Especially if he was being a poo-poo head. When other people are wrong, it's even more important for us to do the right thing." Even if doing the right thing hurt.

When Chloe didn't respond, Brandy asked softly, "Okay?"

"Okay."

"We need to talk about Celestian. I know he seems real to you, but he's only real because you want him to be. He's imaginary to everyone else."

"Really? He's not real?"

"No." And neither was the comforting presence in her dreams. Both were illusions created by needy hearts.

"He looks real." Chloe still wasn't convinced.

"You know how your clothes become too small when you grow?"

"Yes."

"I think you've outgrown Celestian." Brandy would be wise to move on too. To give up her fantasy and get back to her original plan. Find a stay-at-home man to love.

"Like I outgrew my Little Mermaid bathing suit?"

"Exactly like that. Maybe you needed him when we first moved here because you missed Daddy and Grandma and Grandpa and all your friends back home. But we're settled in now. We're happy. You see your daddy and Mallory and your grandparents. You have friends at school and dancing class."

"Trick said he outgrew his dragon."

Brandy swallowed the lump in her throat. Trick had outgrown his need for her, too. "See?"

"I'm not supposed to talk about it, but Celestian came to help you and Trick. If he goes away, how will you and Trick figure stuff out?"

Brandy hugged Chloe close. Did her little girl feel so responsible for her happiness that she had to make up imaginary helpers? Didn't she think her mother could run her own life? What kind of message had Brandy been sending her? "Honey. Trick and I don't need Celestian's help.

256

Trick's been gone because of his work."

"But you're sad when Trick's not here."

"I miss him, but I'm not sad." She hated lying, but Chloe was too young to understand the complicated situation. Sad didn't begin to describe how she felt about what had happened between her and Trick. Her aching heart longed for what would never be.

"Is Trick ever coming back?"

"I'm sure you'll see him again. When he isn't so busy."

"You promise?"

"Yes." Brandy didn't make promises she couldn't keep, but this time stretching the truth seemed necessary.

"I wish Trick were here right now," Chloe murmured. "He would take care of us."

Brandy tipped up her daughter's chin, and then pointed to the cartoon character logo on her pajama top. "You and I? We're strong like Powerpuff Girls. We can take care of ourselves. So you inform Celestian we have matters under control and no longer require his assistance."

Chloe's eyes widened. "You mean tell him to go back to where he came from?"

"I think that would be best."

"Okay." Chloe slid to the floor and solemnly held the door. "This won't be easy. Can I have some privacy, please?"

"Certainly. Tell me when you're done, and I'll come and tuck you in."

Brandy stood in the hall and pressed her ear against Chloe's closed door. Tears filled her eyes as she listened to her little girl say goodbye to part of her childhood. Her baby was growing up. Facing a reality that had tripped up her mother so often. Chloe needed to learn the difference between real and imaginary, but Brandy was sorry she couldn't hold on to her fantasies a little longer.

Reality was tough. Life was hard. Chloe would learn soon enough that she couldn't always wish things into being the way she wanted. And neither could her mother.

"You have to go now." Inside her room, Chloe paused as though listening to the other side of an argument.

"I don't know where. Home. The moon. The brightest star. Wherever you lived before you came here."

"I don't know what banish means. But you have to go."

"Because we have . . . matters under control."

"How do *you* know? Maybe they *are* ready to be on their own."

"Trick's just busy. He *did not* leave us because you aren't telling him to be here any more."

"I know because I'm big now. I'm five and a half. I can take care of myself."

"That doesn't matter. Mommy wants you to go."

"Yes. So do I. I want you to go too."

"Maybe it is most irregular, but I'm the boss, and you can't argue with me. Goodbye Celestian. Thank you for your help, but we can do this by ourselves."

"I hope we can have a happy ending without you, too."

After a few more moments of silence, the door creaked open. Chloe stood there in her pink PJs, looking drained and tired and much smaller than she had only minutes before. Giving up her fantasy had taken a lot out of her. Brandy knew exactly how she felt.

"Is Celestian gone?" Brandy asked.

"I think so." Chloe looked around the room. Behind the curtains. Under the bed. In the closet. When she finished searching, she wrapped her arms around Brandy and buried her face against her mother's stomach. Her thin shoulders shook with the force of her sobs. "I made him go away. He can't come back. Celestian is gone for ever and ever."

H.A.R.P. Emergency Communiqué
From: Mission Control
To: Celestian, Earthbound Operative
Mission: Operation True Love
Subject: Recall Order

ALERT! System protocol has hereby been breached. Mission aborted. Operative is ordered to communicate current whereabouts and status. Required termination documentation must be filed within twelve hours of tactical failure. Report to command center immediately to initiate debriefing procedures or face charges of dereliction of duty.

Operative will be isolated in time-out until such time as a special review panel can be convened to determine disposition of operative's fate.

H.A.R.P. Field Report
From: Celestian, Operative in Limbo
To: Mission Control
Subject: Operation True Love

Progress Report: Arrival imminent. Mission deemed impossible from initial undertaking. Further intervention prohibited by current conditions and rejection of operative by assigned human. Satisfactory completion of operation no longer possible.

Repeat: Outcome no longer favorable. All is lost!

Conclusions: Knowledge gained from field experience reinforces operative's hypothesis that unsupervised human beings are incapable of finding true love, even when it is right before their eyes.

Project Summary: Happy endings are indeed miracles.

Chapter Twelve

"How was Houston?" Brandy handed Trick the cup of black coffee he'd requested. Not that he needed caffeine. He was already moving at warp speed. He'd raced past her desk, slowing down only long enough to give her a quick peck on the cheek.

"Is that where I've been? The past few days have been a blur." He looked up from the mail that had accumulated during his absence and grinned. Despite the demands of his business, he didn't look harried or stressed. In fact, he looked wonderful. Working outdoors, he'd kept his summer tan well into autumn. Despite late nights and early mornings, he seemed energized. Well rested. Why shouldn't he? His dream hadn't turned into disappointment. Amazing what a steady infusion of adrenaline did for a man.

She placed several letters on his desk for his signature. He scribbled his name without bothering to read the contents and handed them back. He'd flown in from the offshore drilling site and was scheduled to meet Charles at the courthouse. He still refused to consider a settlement in the lawsuit, so he and Harry Peet were giving their depositions today.

"What time did you get in?" The question could be interpreted as casual interest. He didn't need to know that she'd sat up until nearly midnight waiting for his call and then had taken the phone to bed with her, just in case.

"Late. Sometime after two." He quickly sorted the mail into two stacks, dropped one in a desk drawer and the other in the trash. "I would have called, but I didn't want to wake you. Thanks for holding down the fort while I was gone. I couldn't maintain this crazy pace without you."

Great. Now she was an enabler. "Just doing my job." Not too long ago, she'd believed he valued more than her ability to balance accounts and juggle appointments. Now she wasn't so sure. She still hadn't told him about Charles' offer. She hadn't found anyone to take over as office manager. That was her excuse. The truth was, she couldn't make up her mind. She had no doubts about working for Charles. She would enjoy handling the defense cases.

Leaving Trick was the problem.

If he broke off with her, working at Hotspur might be her only chance to see him. On the other hand, if she had a separate life, it wouldn't hurt so much to be shut out of his. A third option focused on the positive instead of the negative. Working elsewhere would make things easier if they decided to take their relationship to the next level.

Okay. So she couldn't give up on him completely. She was only human.

The phone rang. Brandy answered and handed him the receiver.

"Charles. What's up?" Trick frowned as he listened to his lawyer. "Sure. See you then." He ended the call. "I'm sorry, I have to rush off. There are a few things Charles wants to go over before we meet with Peet and Futterman."

"I thought he'd already prepped you for the deposition."

"He has, but something else has come up. I was hoping we could have dinner tonight, but I need to check on the crew when I'm done at the courthouse. They're capping a little blowout over in your neck of the woods. One of Chaco Petroleum's wells near Slapdown."

"I know. I took the call." She smiled. "I work here, remember?"

"And I count my blessings for that every

day. How about dinner tomorrow night?" He grimaced. "No, wait, tomorrow is Thursday. That won't work. Maybe by this weekend, things will slow down."

"Maybe." She couldn't help thinking he preferred things speeded up. Maybe she'd been wrong thinking he understood there was more to life than work. "Don't forget. I won't be in the office Friday. Ace said he'd stand in for me and answer the phones."

"Did you tell me that?"

"Twice. Remember? I'm helping out at Chloe's school that day." A month ago, when she'd asked for the day off to head up the Fall Festival decorating committee, he'd told her to consider it a paid "personal day."

"No problem." He grabbed the Stetson he'd tossed on the credenza and headed for the door. Checked his watch. Muttered an oath. "I have to go."

"I understand." Talking to her was not on his agenda today. She followed him into the outer office where he stopped to answer his jangling cell phone. Clients had no trouble reaching him. If she were on fire, maybe she could snag his attention.

But what would she say? Trick had work on his mind. Important work. Complaining about him not calling her last night seemed petty compared to saving hundreds of thousands of dollars worth of fossil fuel for a grateful nation. She was no high-maintenance, clingy female. Making selfish demands of the man she loved wasn't her style. However, she wouldn't mind discussing the future. One they may or may not be sharing.

The anxiety of not knowing where she stood with Trick brought all of Brandy's old insecurities flooding back. As a child, she'd walked into one new school after another, never knowing what to expect. Happy in the morning could mean miserable by nightfall. During her brief marriage, Joe's unstable moods had been a constant source of uncertainty. Amazing highs followed by numbing lows. She'd been trapped on an emotional roller coaster the entire time they'd lived together.

Trick was a different kind of thrill ride. One day she was convinced they were meant to be together. That they were destiny's darlings, blessed to find love so rare it came around only once in a lifetime. The next she wasn't sure he remembered she existed. As much as she loved Trick, she could no longer live in limbo. She would make herself crazy wondering if she and Chloe had a place in his life. She needed predictability. Chloe needed stability. The thought of riding another roller coaster made her queasy. For her daughter's sake and her own peace of mind, she needed to keep her feet on the ground.

Trick finished his call, dropped the phone into his pocket and headed for the door as if determined not to let another delay slow him down. "I'll call you when I get a chance."

When he didn't have anything better to do. She bit back the retort. This was not the time, and the office was not the place. Trick liked to keep his personal and professional lives separate. He would not appreciate her flinging her fears at him on the way out. She might not have much, but she had pride. And it wouldn't let her beg for reassurance in the parking lot.

He paused at the door, turned and strode back to her. Cupping her face in his hands, he kissed her again. No quick peck this time. His slow, deep caress touched more than her lips. It touched her soul. Her heart. There was a powerful, unspoken message in his kiss. Had she imagined the doubts that only moments ago seemed so real? She longed to melt in his arms. To become a part of him he couldn't leave behind. The part he couldn't live without.

He reluctantly dragged his lips from hers. "I gotta go. Charles said it was important." Halfway out the door, he asked, "Oh, by the way, how's Chloe?"

It hurt to think her daughter was only an afterthought to Trick. It would hurt even more if Chloe ever figured out where she stood among his priorities. "She's fine." She wasn't, of course, but he was about to face a man who was suing him. He didn't need to hear about a five-year-old's problems.

Chloe had been quiet and broody since giving up Celestian. She missed her imaginary friend, but she'd vowed he was gone and wouldn't return. Trick wasn't a parent and didn't know how easily a child's tender heart could be crushed. To a little girl, promises were magical things, not to be broken.

"Give her a hug for me." He waved as he walked away. "Tell her we'll go to Mister Cheesie's again soon."

Don't make more promises you can't keep, she warned silently.

Brandy finished the computerized billing. There was something to be said about work's power to keep a worried mind occupied. A couple of hours later, the front door opened. She looked up and greeted the visitor. The older woman didn't look like a typical Hotspur customer but in Texas, you never knew who might own an oil well.

"May I help you?" she asked with a smile.

"You must be Brandy." The tiny woman spoke with the slow cadence of the Deep South, her drawl more plantation than plains. Her handshake was deceptively firm, her gray eyes youthful and bright. She had the tanned athleticism of a pro golfer and wore her short sun-streaked blond hair in a stylish bob. She was sixty if she was a day, but her denim skirt and colorful Western shirt made Brandy think she would reject the senior citizen label.

"Yes. Brandy Mitchum."

"Aren't you just the cutest thing? Pleased to meet you, Brandy. I'm Wylodene Davis, née Talbott. You can call me Wylo, like the tree. I used to work here. For about half a century."

"Of course. Trick told me all about you."

"I'll just bet he has." She winked. "Don't listen to him. Most of what he says about me probably isn't true. That boy got his tighty-whities in a wad when I succumbed to romance. Lordy! All I did was run off and get married." Wylo waved her hand in a gesture as dramatic as her tone. "You'd have thought I killed his talking pig and ruined his chance to join the circus."

Forthright and funny, Wylo had been an important person in Trick's life. Brandy could see why. "He'll be sorry he missed you. He's gone for the day."

"That's too bad. How about Ace? Is that old war dog around?"

"No, the whole crew is on a call-out."

"Mind if I sit down?" Wylodene settled into the chair. Clad in fringed boots, her tiny feet barely brushed the floor. "How's Trick doing these days?"

"Great."

"Business all right?"

"Booming."

"Glad to hear it. Maybe he'll finally let up. Wouldn't hurt him to run on cruise control for a while instead of overdrive."

"What do you mean?"

"Shoot! Trick's been pushing himself ever since Buck was killed in that oil well explosion. You know about that?"

"Yes, he told me." All she knew was that

Buck Templeton had died during Trick's first trip overseas.

"His mother died years before, when he was just a little fella," Wylodene continued. "Hotspur was all he had left of his parents. He swore to keep the company going. To make it mean something. A legacy to his father, I guess. Or maybe a memorial. He was just a kid, but he worked harder than ten men."

Brandy sighed. "He still does."

"I know. That's always been a sore spot between us. I used to tell him regular as clockwork: Get a life, Templeton!"

"What did he say to that?"

"What do you think? Mind your own business, Talbott!" Wylo gave Brandy a sly look. "I'm hoping maybe you can help him in that regard. Offer him some diversion, perhaps?"

Brandy's cheeks warmed. If she were to guess the source of the woman's information, she'd start at the beginning of the alphabet. Ace. "I do what I can."

"Good for you. Don't give up on Trick. Under all that bluster and fear, he's a good man."

"Fear?" Brandy was incredulous. "Trick's the most fearless man I ever met."

"Oh, he'll risk his life without blinking."

The older woman lowered her voice. "But he's terrified of risking his heart."

"Not much I can do about that." Brandy couldn't believe she was discussing something as personal as her love life with a stranger, but Wylodene didn't seem like a stranger. More like a window. Through which she could see Trick more clearly.

"Poor boy. He hasn't been trained properly. Women ought to take pointers from the Army when it comes to shaping men into husbands."

"The Army?"

"You know what they do with raw recruits, right? They tear them down so they can build them up again. The right way."

"I don't know about that. Trick's pretty set in his ways."

"When it comes to men, nothing's etched in stone until they're buried under one. They can change. They just need the right inspiration. Which brings us to you, dear. How do you like working here?"

"Why do you ask?"

"Curiosity. You know, the weirdest thing happened to me. I woke up one morning last week, Tuesday I think it was. Or maybe Wednesday. Anyway, I woke up and I thought, Wylo, you need to get over to Hotspur and talk to that gal. I'd heard about you, but something told me we needed to meet."

"Really?"

"Strange isn't it?" She opened her handbag and pulled out a tin of cinnamon-flavored mints. "Want one? I don't know why, but I set in craving these things right around the time I started thinking about coming here."

Brandy accepted a mint and popped it into her mouth. The cinnamon flavor was strong, recalling other strange, cinnamon-related incidents. "May I ask why you didn't come last week?"

"I don't remember. Something must have come up. Not that my life's a whirl-wind of social engagements, but my old man probably distracted me. The feeling that I should come here has been on me all week. Then today, I reached in my purse, saw those mints, and thought of you again. Isn't that just the most mysterious thing? I sure hope it's not a sign of senility. They say you don't miss your mind once it's gone, but I don't want to test that theory."

Brandy laughed. "I'm sure it isn't. I love cinnamon, too." However, she hadn't felt the same cravings lately and had switched back to diet cola. Even Chloe had stopped asking for cinnamon toast for breakfast.

"I hate to think I drove all the way over here on account of a mint. You want to talk to me about anything?"

Did she? Was Wylodene's unexpected appearance today a sign telling her to accept Charles' job offer? The attorney had thought of her when he'd eaten a scone. A cinnamon scone. Another coincidence? There'd been a lot of those in her life since she'd moved to town. Even more since she met Trick.

Everything happened for a reason. Maybe Wylo was here for a reason, too. Who better to take over as manager than the woman who'd organized the office in the first place? "Are you employed anywhere at the moment?"

"Heavens no! Who'd hire a fossil like me? Gal my age would screw up the group benefits." She sighed wistfully. "I do miss working though. Some ladies may find spending the day at the bingo hall stimulating, but it's one long yawn for me. I like a little more excitement in my life than B14."

"Would you consider going back to work?"

Wylo perked up, suddenly interested. "You bet your bloomers, I would. That new husband of mine is retired. You know what that means?"

"You could use the money?" Brandy suggested.

"No. It means he's home all the time. Twenty-four-piddling-around-hours a day. I love him, but I don't want to be his only hobby."

Brandy folded her arms on the desk. The implications were clear. She'd reached a fork in her journey and had a decision to make. If Wylo took over at Hotspur, Brandy and Trick would be free.

The question remained, would they be free to grow closer? Or free to grow apart? She didn't know what the future would bring, but either way, working elsewhere was the key to making *something* happen.

"Hypothetically speaking," she said to Wylodene, "if the right job opened up, say your old position here at Hotspur, you would consider taking it?"

"Would I?" Wylo slapped her knees and a wide smile deepened the sun-carved furrows beside her mouth. "Only as fast as a hypothetical hound dog would snap up a hypothetical pork chop if the right one came along."

"Honey, I don't think he's coming this time." Brandy placed her hand on her daughter's shoulder, offering what little

275

consolation she could. Chloe was decked out in fairy finery for the Fall Festival. Her little girl looked adorable dressed in a pink fairy princess costume, complete with sparkly slippers, magic wand and glittery, bobbing antenna. She'd been anxiously watching out the front window for half an hour. "We should probably go. You don't want to be late for the festival."

"He'll come," she said resolutely. "He said he would."

Brandy wore a gypsy outfit for her stint in the fortune telling booth. She lifted her voluminous skirts and kneeled down to her daughter's level. "I don't remember inviting Trick. I don't think he knows about the festival."

"He knows. I asked him. The day I got the pumpkins with Daddy. I told him about the cakewalk and the games and the prizes. I told him I had to wear a costume, but he didn't. Trick said he wouldn't miss it. He promised."

"In that case, I'm sure he would be here if something important hadn't come up." The last time Brandy had heard from Trick was a quick phone call Wednesday night before he drove to Dallas for a breakfast meeting the next day. She'd worked with the decorating committee today, carving pumpkins and stuffing scarecrows. Spent the afternoon draping fake spiderwebs and stringing crepe paper streamers around the elementary school gym. She'd kept her cell phone handy in case he called, but he hadn't.

"He'll come," Chloe insisted with a believer's faith. "What's more important than a promise?"

To a child, nothing. To a man as driven as Trick, almost anything. Brandy drew her daughter close for a hug. What could she tell her to soften the disappointment? How could she make Chloe understand what was going on with Trick, when she didn't understand herself?

"Don't smoosh my wings," Chloe cautioned.

"I won't. Come on, baby. Let's go. We want to get to the cafeteria before they run out of food. They're serving pizza and hot dogs. And green goblin juice."

Chloe wasn't tempted. "I'm not hungry. Daddy used to not come, too."

"You remember that?" Chloe was only three when Joe finally developed parenting skills. Prior to his life-changing event, he'd been an inconsiderate, inconsistent father. He'd often missed court-appointed visitation, leaving poor little Chloe feeling unloved and rejected. Brandy had always made excuses for his no-shows. Not to make him look better. To make her daughter feel better.

"You said Daddy was busy." An accusation.

"I can't believe you remember that. It happened so long ago."

"I have a good memory."

"Yes, but you shouldn't worry about the past. Think about the future instead. Let's go to the carnival and have fun. Maybe you can win us a plate of black cat cupcakes at the cakewalk."

"All those times when Daddy didn't come?" Chloe skewered her with a gaze so unflinching it would see through any remedial lies she could tell. "He wasn't busy, was he? I bet he forgot about me."

"Yes, sometimes he did forget. He never forgets now. You can count on your daddy to always be there for you."

"I know." Chloe looked up at Brandy, her wide eyes glistening with tears. She wiped them away before they spilled over and ruined her fairy princess face paint. "Did Trick forget?"

"Probably," she answered honestly. She wanted to believe Trick would have made good on his promise had he remembered.

"He wouldn't stand you up on purpose."

"Celestian was right. I shouldn't have made him go away." Chloe flung herself down on the couch. She didn't even care if she smooshed her wings. "I want Celestian, and I want Trick!"

With her own heart as tattered as Chloe's fairy wings, Brandy tried to soothe her distraught child. She knew better than anyone you didn't always get what you wanted.

Chapter Thirteen

Sunday afternoon rolled around, and Trick still hadn't called. Brandy got a recorded message when she dialed his cell number. *The customer you are trying to reach is currently out of range.* She sighed. A hi-tech way of letting her know he was also out of her league. She made sure her cell unit was charged, and then checked to see if the house phone was working properly. It was. If he wanted to get in touch with her, he could.

"Hey, I have an idea." She needed to occupy her mind almost as much as she needed to provide a diversion for the still-moping Chloe. "Why don't we take down the Halloween decorations and put our turkey pilgrim on the porch? Thanksgiving will be here before you know it."

Chloe looked up from her drawing and shrugged. She was still wearing the glitter-coated bobble antenna from her fairy costume. "If you want to."

"Afterward, we can go to the library and check out books."

"I don't think so." She bent over the crayoned picture of a house.

Her daughter's current lack of interest was a bad sign. To Chloe every day was special, but holidays were the most special of all. Brandy made sure she had fond memories and traditions. They read holiday-themed books together, prepared special foods and cruised discount sales for colorful decorations. They weren't Irish, but at the Mitchum house, even St. Patrick's Day was a big enough deal to warrant a shamrock-studded wreath on the door.

"You haven't eaten any candy." Chloe had ended yesterday's trick or treating expedition after visiting houses on only one side of the block. She hadn't wanted to be out too long in case Trick showed up.

She shrugged again. "Candy's bad for your teeth."

Hard to work up much enthusiasm for treats when her favorite Trick was conspicuously absent. Chloe would have plenty of future opportunities to be upset over a man. Five was too young to start. Brandy could deal with her own feelings, but she wouldn't allow Trick's actions to negatively affect her child.

"Let's go outside. We need some fresh

air and sunshine." She helped Chloe into a sweater and pulled on her own jacket, tucking the cell phone in a pocket. At least she knew she was pathetic in her optimism.

They took down the string of orange lights and stashed the straw-filled scarecrow in the garage. When it came time to dispose of the rotting pumpkins, Chloe regarded the big jack-o'-lantern Trick had carved with a solemn expression. The artful vegetable was well past its expiration date.

"The smile used to be big and happy," she pointed out. "Now it's sad and smooshed."

"That's what happens when pumpkins get too ripe," Brandy explained gently.

"I wish it could be happy longer."

"I know, baby. Some things aren't meant to last. We enjoy them while we can, and then we have to say goodbye." Chloe turned away when Brandy dropped the squishy squash into the trash can. It was her fault Chloe was so upset. She never should have let her daughter become attached to a man who couldn't remember the promises he made.

"I wanna ride my bike now." Chloe adjusted her antenna before climbing up on the seat.

"Stay on the sidewalk, please. And come back when you get to the big tree." Chloe pedaled off. Brandy had thought Trick would be the one to take the training wheels off the little pink bike. She'd planned to introduce him to her family at Thanksgiving. Had even imagined him at her side on Christmas morning watching Chloe unwrap gifts. Not exactly reality-based scenarios, they'd grown out of longing and loneliness. The sooner she admitted Trick was one of those good things that had to end too soon, the better.

She pulled out the cell phone and found Charles Thorson's number on speed dial. They exchanged pleasantries, and she apologized for calling him at home. Then she took a deep breath. And a big step. "If that job offer is still on the table, I'd like to take you up on it."

He assured her it was. If only she could be half as pleased as he sounded. All she felt was resignation. When she offered to let him know her starting date tomorrow, he told her he looked forward to working with her. Wylodene Davis was next. She was thrilled at the prospect of returning to her old job but hesitated to accept before discussing the change with Trick.

As office manager, Brandy was authorized to hire support staff, and Wylodene agreed to come in the next day to fill out the necessary paperwork. She wouldn't need any training. A few hours of review would bring her up to speed. Brandy would stay for a couple of days during the transition, and have the rest of the week to get her wayward emotions under control.

As if a few days would be long enough to accomplish that task.

She raked errant leaves in a pile and dragged the trash can to the curb. Might as well leave her crumpled hopes and dreams beside it. Dreams. Troublesome little things. She'd taken an over-the-counter sleep aid last night. She'd slept soundly, and the dream had been vivid. When the Midnight Man arrived, she'd gotten up, walked to the window, opened it and turned her back. When she looked again, he'd been gone, and she knew he was gone for good. The assurance didn't make her feel any better.

She straightened the lid on the trash can. Twilight descended early in November, and the light was fading fast. Why did beginnings take so long when endings came too soon?

"Chloe! Time to put away your bike."

They walked toward the house holding

hands. Chloe stopped and gazed up at the purple velvet sky. After several moments, she smiled for the first time in days. "I think heaven must be a very nice place."

"So do I." Brandy's hand rested on her daughter's shoulder.

"See that sparkly star up there?" Chloe stretched one arm, pointing to the first light flickering overhead.

"Yes."

"I think that's where Celestian lives. I think he's looking down and smiling at me right now."

"Why is he smiling?"

"Because Trick is coming home."

Four days later, Trick parked his truck in front of Brandy's house. It was after ten o'clock, but a single light in the window told him she might still be awake. He had to see her. Hold her. Exhausted from fighting fires in a remote area of the Yucatan Peninsula, he had never been so glad to get home.

Home. His all-expense-paid trip to hell had taught him a valuable lesson. Home wasn't a place. It had nothing to do with sheltering walls or the roof overhead. Home was the person who thought about you when you were gone. Who missed you and welcomed you and warmed you until you had to go back out into the cold. He'd never had a real home before.

But he had one now.

Brandy opened the door, dressed in a heavy robe and slippers. Long hair loose around her shoulders, sweet face bare of makeup, she smelled like the bubbles she poured in Chloe's tub. It was all he could do not to sweep her into his arms. The house was quiet, illuminated by a reading lamp. One of the courtroom novels she loved lay upside down on the chair she'd just vacated.

When he'd been far away, fighting fires in the jungle, he'd dreamed about this moment. This place. This woman. For the first time in his life, he hadn't thought about the next adventure. He'd thought only of home.

"Trick? What are you doing here?" Obviously surprised to see him, Brandy stepped aside and let him in. He was lousy at gauging the emotions of others, but if he wasn't mistaken, she was glad to see him.

"I never told you, did I?" He'd waited long enough.

"Told me what?"

He was such an idiot. He gave himself a mental smack on the head. "I can't believe

I never said the words. I thought them. A hundred times a day. I should have told you. I meant to tell you. But I was so busy making sure I had something to offer that I forgot."

"Trick, what are you talking about?"

He stepped to the couch, pulled her down beside him and held both her hands in his. "I should have told you before. In my own defense, my only excuse is lack of experience. Better late than never, right?" He lifted her hands to his lips and kissed them. "I love you, Brandy. I love you."

She gasped. Like someone in shock, whose top priority was making her stopped heart beat again, she couldn't seem to free up enough energy to speak. Well, that wasn't exactly the reaction he'd expected. She blinked. Swallowed. Cleared her throat. Nothing. She had nothing for him. No joy. No relief. No, "I love you, too, Trick." Should he have brought smelling salts? The way she was staring at him, he could have said, "I come from a galaxy far, far away."

He was no expert at professing undying love, but he didn't think he would fail so miserably. "Brandy?"

Her response was a slowly lifted index finger. It was shaking. Then it jabbed him in the chest. When she finally spoke, her words sounded as if they'd been wrung through the wringer of her soul. "Don't. Don't you dare tell me you love me."

"What?" Now it was his turn to be shocked. Weren't those the three magic words that opened the door to the kingdom of happiness?

"Don't tell me you love me." She sucked in a deep breath. "Unless you mean it. *I* mean it, Trick. Don't."

Relief flooded through him, leaching some of the tension from his muscles. He grinned. Okay, those *were* the magic words. "I never say anything I don't mean." He drew her close. A kiss would seal the deal, but she slipped out of his embrace and moved away to the opposite end of the couch.

Again, not the reaction he'd anticipated when plotting this scene out in his mind from a tent in the Yucatan. He'd finally worked up enough raw courage to jump into the deep end of the commitment pool, and the woman of his dreams was back-paddling away from him. Not too promising. "Brandy. Talk to me. What did I do wrong?"

She finally got her voice back. It was squeaky and weak, but audible. "I love you, too, Trick."

Now that was more like it. He reached for her again.

Again, she pulled back. "I love you, and that's why I'm letting you go."

He frowned. Maybe he was strung out from too much caffeine and too little sleep, but those two sentiments did not fit together. "I don't understand."

"The past couple of weeks taught me something." She stood up and wrapped her arms around her middle. Paced in a tight circle. The frightened-doe expression was back. Not quite the glowing look of love he'd been going for.

"Me, too." He needed a connection and reached for her, but she sidestepped him.

"Please, just let me say this. I'm nervous, and it's hard enough without you destroying what little willpower I have."

"I'm listening. But sit down. You're making *me* nervous."

She settled on the couch beside him, but not too close. "For a while, I thought we were meant to be together. All the signs were there."

"Signs. That's right."

"No. That's wrong. I think we may be, for lack of a better term, star-crossed lovers."

Trick racked his mind to find a reference

that would make the term relevant. "Star-crossed? Like Romeo and Juliet?"

She nodded. "No matter how much we think we love each other, how much it feels like we're soul mates —"

"You feel that, too?" He took her hand again. "I thought it was just me."

"No matter how much we think we love each other," she continued impatiently, "our stars are on a different trajectory. I need things like security and stability. The certainty that you'll always be there for me and Chloe."

Trick knew he could give her those things, but she didn't. As much as he wanted to take charge of the situation and trivialize her doubts, he couldn't be the boss here. Her concerns were legitimate, and unless he convinced her he had changed, he would never get the chance to prove it. Their future was on the line. The moment could explode in his face if he didn't cap her runaway fears. It was up to him.

"Why do you think I've been working so hard lately?" he asked.

She slumped in frustration. Or was it confusion? "Because like a shark, you are genetically programmed to be constantly on the move? To look for the next big thing?"

"No!" She'd compared him to a shark. That hurt. But she did have reason to condemn his actions. He'd spent a lifetime doing exactly what she accused him of doing. "I mean, yes. You're right. I have done that. But since meeting you, I've been moving for a different reason. Toward you. It took being isolated in a burning jungle to make me realize why I was pushing so hard."

"Why, Trick?" Her soft words were full of challenge.

Everything was riding on his answer. "So I could be worthy of you. I want to deserve your love and shoulder the burdens you've carried so long. I want to take care of you and Chloe. Show you the world and give you a nice life to come home to. I don't know how to say it any plainer, Brandy. I love you, and I want to spend the rest of my days with you."

"Trick." Brandy's hands tightened into fists and clutched the loose chenille fabric of her bathrobe. She was losing her grip, slipping back into thunderstruck modality. Trick was saying all the right things, everything she'd longed to hear. So what was the problem?

She'd fantasized about his return. She'd practiced the name Brandy Templeton in her head, just to see how it sounded. Chloe had created an imaginary playmate, but she was guilty of creating an imaginary husband that couldn't possibly fulfill all her stringent requirements.

Flattened by an unsettling mix of emotions, Brandy collapsed against the couch cushions. She'd been afraid she'd never hear the words from Trick. Now that she had, she didn't dare believe them. She'd daydreamed about the perfect husband, and now a wonderful man was offering to play the part. What was wrong with her that she couldn't let go of her fantasies long enough to let him?

If reality couldn't live up to imagination, it would be worse than never knowing true love. Wouldn't it?

"Brandy, listen to me." Trick grasped her upper arms, and held her gaze with his. "I want to give you the rest of my life. Chloe's smart enough to get into Harvard. I want to give her that. And someday, I want to give her the fairy-tale wedding little girls dream about. Anything she wants."

Lulled by the heat of Trick's touch, Brandy jerked at the mention of Chloe's name. This wasn't just about her. She had to think of her little girl. Trick's words had swept some of the past's debris from her heart, but that didn't mean he could move in.

"What she wanted was for you to take her to the Fall Festival. To play silly games and eat cupcakes. A college education isn't relevant to a five-year-old, Trick. Pin the Hat on the Witch is. Do you have any idea how devastated she was when you didn't show?"

"I don't understand."

"She told me you promised to take her to the school carnival. She stood by the window for half an hour. Waiting for you."

"Damn!" His face crumpled and he threw back his head and groaned. "Oh, no! Poor kid. I know how she felt. God knows I waited for my parents often enough. I wouldn't wish that feeling on anyone. Especially not Chloe. Was she really upset?"

"Yes."

"Nothing I can say can take away that pain. But you have to know I'd never intentionally do anything to hurt Chloe. I was already in Mexico by then. Why didn't you tell her what happened?"

"I didn't find out about the Yucatan call-out until Monday. I didn't work Friday because I was at the school. Helping decorate for the carnival."

"I completely forgot." Panic filled his eyes. "Will she forgive me?"

"She already has. Little girls are eternal optimists."

He squeezed her arm. "What about you? Can you forgive me?"

"Big girls are realists. I've left Hotspur."

"I know. I called the office from the airport and Wylo told me you'd taken a job with Charles."

"And you're not upset?"

"I might have been, had I known you were giving up on more than your job at Hotspur." He paused, and Brandy could almost see the wheels turning in his head.

Trick chose his next words carefully. Being clueless about women and their emotional needs was definitely a disadvantage. He'd played most of his hold cards and still had no idea whether he could convince Brandy to take a chance on him. He was asking a lot from a woman who'd gambled before and lost.

"Charles can give you the kind of work you've always wanted to do," he said. "I thought I made it clear from the beginning that you could take a paralegal job if you found one."

"I was afraid you'd see my defection as another abandonment."

"Whoa." Gut-check time. Nothing was quite as terrifying as being slapped in the face by his worst fear. Even if he didn't want to hear the truth, Trick had to ask the question. He had to know if Brandy could walk away. If she would. "You *aren't* abandoning me, are you? Because I can't let that happen."

"There's one lesson you haven't learned," she said with a soft sigh.

"What's that?"

"You can't always be in control."

"I haven't been in control for one minute since I wiped that chocolate off your face on the road." He smiled, hoping to coax one from her. *Please, gimme something to go on here.*

"I'm sorry." Her sadly resigned expression was that of a mourner at a funeral. He wouldn't give up. Quitting wasn't his style. There was no blowout too big it couldn't be capped. If she was grieving the death of their love, he still had a chance.

She drew a long breath, as if she needed extra wind to propel her words. "We're too different. It would take a lot of compromise to make a relationship work. You're better at fighting than seeing the other side of an argument."

"I'm learning about compromise. Futterman called Charles the day of the deposition and offered to take a smaller settlement for his client. For the first time in my life, I realized that I didn't have to be right. You taught me to look outside myself. I sat in that room and really listened to Harry Peet's complaint. He's still a flake, but he made some valid points."

"And?" The spark of trust that lit her eyes warmed Trick's heart.

"I authorized Charles to settle for a tenth of their original claim. For some reason, fighting just didn't seem worth it. I don't want to be tied up in court. I want to be with you."

Fighting wasn't worth it? Maybe he could learn to compromise. Brandy slid back down the couch, stopping close enough to take his big hand in both of hers. She was right to liken Trick to a thrill ride. She'd traveled from heartbreak to hope in five minutes. "You don't think we're too different?"

"On the surface, we seem like opposites. However, if you plot out our differences, you'll see that together, we form a whole. We're both sides of the coin." He'd obviously spent a lot of time thinking about their situation. About her. His enthusiasm increased. "We're made for each other. I'll help you explore new horizons, and you'll make a home for us to return to. Alone, neither of us could be what we were meant to be. Together we can be anything we want."

Brandy wanted to believe. She'd always wanted to believe. From the first fateful moment when she'd glimpsed her future in Trick's eyes, she'd sensed destiny at work. If only she had Chloe's faith, she wouldn't be so afraid of reality spoiling illusion. "This is important. I need to know. Are you sure you want to settle down?"

A wide, slow smile creased his face. He couldn't beam with such confidence if he didn't know the answer to her question. "I've never been more sure of anything. You made me want a connection and made me believe it could last forever. Take a chance, Brandy. On me. On us. Love is the biggest adventure of all, and I can't wait to get started." His kiss burned away her reservations, sending her worries up in smoke as a new fire kindled in her heart. This fire would warm her forever.

"The signs were there all along." Brandy leaned into Trick. "Think about all those chance meetings. The strange coincidences that got me fired and even stranger one that led me to Hotspur. If we'd really looked, it's all there, laid out like a cosmic map."

"The map of a road going in only one direction." He held her in a sheltering embrace. "I guess that's why I remained a bachelor for so long. I was waiting for you."

"Maybe that's why my marriage to Joe didn't work out," she whispered. "I was waiting for you."

"It's a heck of a theory."

"And a lot to risk on faith."

"I've been a fighter all my life," he said. "But even I know better than to fight fate."

They heard a giggle and turned to see Chloe standing in the doorway in her pajamas. They smiled at each other and welcomed the child into the circle of their arms.

Snuggling close, Chloe giggled again and looked heavenward. "See, Celestian. I *told* you we could do it without you."

Epilogue

The After Place

"I wish to return to earth, sirs." Celestian stood firm in the quiet stillness of the interview room, braced for the Placement Committee's reaction.

"We are confused by your unusual request, Celestian." The senior saint chairing the committee expressed the concerns of the entire panel. "We've called you here today to explain."

That could be difficult. As much thought as he'd given his decision, Celestian wasn't sure he knew the words to make them understand.

"Even though you were forced to abort your mission, the operation concluded successfully," the senior saint reminded him. "Mission Control is convinced you learned a valuable lesson. Therefore, you're entitled to resume your previous duties as time-out monitor in accordance with the terms of the original offer."

"I am grateful, but I have to go back."

For the first time, Celestian was genuinely patient. There was too much at stake not to be.

"You wish to walk into another life?" asked a committee member.

"No, sir." This would be the hard part. "I want to resume mortal form."

"Mortal form?" The shocked question told Celestian his request was unheard of.

"Resuming mortal form is a backward step in spiritual evolvement," the senior saint pointed out.

A third member spoke. "According to our notes, you 'strongly objected' to being sent to earth for your last assignment."

"That is true."

"And yet now you are willing to return?"

More than willing. He was desperate. "Yes. I want to experience the remainder of the life I lost."

"For what reason?"

"Love, sir."

"Love?" all three committee members asked in unison.

"My recent assignment taught me that true love gives meaning to life. As you know, I died prematurely on my first jaunt to earth. I was deemed unready for return and have resided in The After Place ever since. More than three centuries. I want to go back. I want to fall in love. Sirs."

"Your request is most irregular."

"I didn't see my assignment to its conclusion. But I was instrumental in helping soul mates residing in antipodean personalities overcome their differences long enough to embrace their true feelings. I corrected the original assignment error. Because of my efforts, or in spite of them, harmony was restored in two lives. Three if you count the child. Speaking of which, my task would have been much simpler had I known the spirit of Trick Templeton's late grandmother had reupped as Chloe Mitchum."

"That was need-to-know information. You did fine without it."

"And so I respectfully ask that my request be granted."

"Please wait while the committee reaches a decision."

Placed on cosmic hold, Celestian sat on a bench in the interview chamber and listened to tranquil harp music, interrupted periodically by a soothing female voice relaying a daily tip for maintaining spiritual well-being. All that serenity did little to calm his anxiety.

After what seemed like an eternity, the music clicked off and the committee chairman spoke. "Celestian, we are happy to report that your request has been approved by the Supreme Arbiter."

Celestian sighed with relief. "Thank you. When can I go?"

"The discharge order has been filed. The enhancement process has already begun. Report to Debriefing for an exit interview. If you can demonstrate competency in current events and technology, you may leave at that time. Here are your walking papers."

A white portfolio containing his new identity appeared in Celestian's hands. He opened it, amazed by the speed with which the items had been created. A birth certificate, a social security card, family background, educational records and work history. Everything he needed to be a real man.

"Since you elect to return in your last mortal form, we felt it fitting for you to use your former name."

"Thank you." Celestian clutched the walking papers to his chest, which suddenly felt solid. Substantial. Was that a heart he felt beating inside?

"Since the objective of your expedition is to find your own true love, you will be assigned to a destination compatible with that of your soul mate."

"I have a soul mate?" His new heart skipped a beat.

"Of course. Everyone does. You just didn't meet her in your last life. This time around, it will be up to you to find her. And your destiny."

"Don't worry, sir. I will." A wild wave of anticipation surged through Celestian. Love was one thing. But one true love meant only for him? That was an unexpected, miraculous bonus. "I don't know how to express my gratitude. I can only say, thank you."

"You are most welcome," chorused the saints. "Have a nice life, Raleigh Tate."

About the Author

Debrah Morris — When she isn't writing her own novels and reading novels written by others, Debrah teaches novel writing in workshops and a university program. She is also active in a romance writers group.

She used to have hobbies and other interests, but these days her mind is pretty much one-tracked, and fiction is it.

She loves hearing from readers and can be contacted via her Web site: www.debrahmorris.com or at P.O. Box 522, Norman, OK 73070.